Mad as Helen

Books by Susan McBride

SUSAN McBRIDE

Mad as Helen

A RIVER ROAD MYSTERY

WITNESS

IMPULSE

This book is a work of fiction. The characters, incidents, and dialogue are drawn from the author's imagination and are not to be construed as real. Any resemblance to actual events or persons, living or dead, is entirely coincidental.

Excerpt from *Not a Chance in Helen* copyright © 2014 by Susan McBride.

EPub Edition July 2014 ISBN: 9780062359773

Print Edition ISBN: 9780062359780

10 9 8 7 6 5 4 3 2 1

Prologue

THE MINUTE MATTIE Oldbridge unlocked the front door and stepped inside the house, she sensed something was wrong. She set her overnight bag on the floor, looked around, wrinkled up her nose, and sniffed.

The scent of Pine-Sol from a recent cleaning lingered, as did another smell, one that Mattie couldn't pinpoint. Or was it only her imagination acting up, like the arthritis in her elbow?

She'd been gone just one evening, after all, spending the night with her nephew's family in St. Louis. Maybe she was getting dotty in her old age, so comfy in her own home that she didn't enjoy being away even for a brief spell.

Still, she felt wary as she walked through the house, pausing in the living room to let her spectacled gaze roam. The Steuben pieces her Harvey—God rest his soul—had given to her that last Christmas; hadn't she left them on the shelf?

And where were the sterling candlesticks they'd bought in Mexico? She could have sworn they'd been on the mantel when she'd left for the city yesterday at dusk.

She toyed with her wedding band as she headed into the kitchen.

Fingers trembling, she removed the ceramic top from a canister marked SUGAR. She peered inside but saw only a lone rubber band and a bit of dust.

She swallowed, and her eyes widened behind her horned rims.

"Oh, no, oh, no," she murmured as she hurried from one room to the next, discovering objects she'd come to treasure missing from each. Frantically she groped beneath the clothes that filled the upstairs hamper and pulled out her velvet-lined jewelry box. She opened it up.

Empty.

With a whimper, she put it aside.

That strange sensation she'd felt upon entering the house was more than her mind playing tricks. Someone *had* been here during the time she'd been gone. Someone had been in this very room, had stood right where she was now.

The idea of it chilled her from her dove-white head to her sensible shoes.

Without another thought, Mattie got the heck out. Her heart slapping hard against her ribs, she raced the few blocks to Sheriff Biddle's office. Finding him gone, she hurried across the street to the diner where he ate every other afternoon, as all of River Bend knew.

The crowd of heads turned as she entered. A few

friends called out greetings. But Mattie Oldbridge had eyes only for the sheriff. She didn't notice as the room went quiet. She saw only Biddle as he looked up, his lips puckered to greet a soup spoon poised in midair.

"Good God," Mattie croaked for everyone to hear, "I've been robbed!"

"Robbed?" the crowd echoed.

At which point Mattie nodded and burst into tears.

Biddle dropped his spoon with a clatter, the noise loud against the sudden hush, although the silence was brief enough. Voices rose in a garbled rush. Chairs squeaked and plates rattled as the diner came suddenly alive and Mattie was surrounded.

"Move aside, please, move aside."

Parting the gawkers like Moses did the Red Sea, Biddle took Mattie's arm, and she allowed herself to be led away from the pack, out of the diner, across the street, and to his office, where he settled her into the chair across his desk.

"You need some water, Mrs. Oldbridge?"

"No," she tried to say, but the word that emerged seemed little more than a squeak.

"Would you like my handkerchief?"

That Mattie gratefully accepted, bumping up her glasses to dab at her eyes. She watched him through her tears as he perched on his desk, one leg dangling so that she could see a bit of pale skin above black sock.

"You want to tell me what happened?" he said.

Mattie nodded. "Someone was in my house while I was away."

Biddle cocked his head. "Are you sure, ma'am?"

"Y-yes," she stammered, and her eyes filled with tears again. She made a knot of the kerchief with unsteady fingers. "My best things are gone."

Biddle came off his perch, hiked up his pants below an overlarge belly, and went around his desk to sit down. He pulled out a legal pad and then a pencil, wetting the tip of it with his tongue. "Go on."

"My candlesticks from Mexico are missing." Mattie sniffled. "So are my Steuben pieces and a sterling cigarette case."

Biddle nodded as he wrote.

"He even took the cash I kept in the kitchen." She sighed absently. "I've always put aside a few bills for emergencies ever since Harvey passed."

"How much?" he asked.

"Oh, several hundred at least," she guessed.

Biddle let out a low whistle.

"My jewelry's gone, too, Sheriff," she went on, and he glanced up from the paper. "I had it stuffed way down in the bathroom hamper. How did they know?"

Biddle shook his head as he wrote. "I thought I warned you ladies about hiding valuables in the hamper after the break-ins at Mavis White's and Violet Farley's."

Mattie shifted in her chair, clutching the kerchief in her lap. "Well, I'd been putting it there for the past fifteen years, and no one's stolen so much as a hatpin."

"Any sign of forced entry?"

Mattie closed her eyes to better recall but eventually shook her head. "The door was locked," she told him.

"And I use the heavy-duty dead bolt you recommended when you spoke at my women's club last year."

Biddle's chair squeaked as it released his weight. He stood and slapped on his hat. He had the door open before she'd gotten to her feet. "Let's go, ma'am," he told her. "I'd like to take a look for myself."

By the time Mattie's favorite soap opera came on, Biddle had walked the well-tended plot around the house half a dozen times. He'd dusted sills and knobs and the mantel for fingerprints—leaving Mattie with a mess to clean up—only to scratch his head when he was done.

"Who was it, Sheriff?" she asked before he got back into his squad car. "Who took my best things? Who got in through the locks?"

He paused on her porch, his square face grim. "I'd say it's someone who knew what they were doing, ma'am."

At which point Mattie let out a loud sob.

Chapter 1

HELEN EVANS AWOKE with a start.

Hell's bells, she hadn't actually dozed off, had she? The crossword from that morning's *Alton Telegraph* lay in her lap, its squares almost entirely filled with the purple ink she always used precisely for that purpose.

Ah, she remembered now. She'd gotten stuck on a four-letter word for *seabirds*. She'd had the darned thing right there on the tip of her tongue—hang it all, it was in every other puzzle she did!—when she'd put her glasses aside to rub at her eyes, laid back for the briefest of moments, and fell sound asleep.

"Napping," she clucked, "just like an old person."

Which, in fact, she was, according to AARP and all those restaurants that gave her their senior citizens' discounts without even checking her ID.

Well, as they said, getting old was better than the alternative.

Helen slipped her glasses back on and stared down with wrinkled brow at the crossword in her lap. "Erns," she said aloud just as it came to her. "E-R-N-S," she spelled and filled in the gap she'd been studying before she'd taken her catnap. All right, so her mind might've slowed a bit over the years, but it was still all there.

"If you rest, you rust," as she'd heard someone say once, and Helen felt the same. She wasn't about to let any part of her corrode like a metal lawn chair left out in the rain too often.

Her puzzles and bridge games, the quilts she was forever cross-stitching, each kept her too busy to ponder if her bones were turning brittle or if her brain cells were retiring one by one.

Quickly, she finished up the rest of the crossword, setting the folded newspaper aside with a satisfied sigh when she was done.

She removed her specs and glanced up. Through the screens that fenced in her porch, she saw Amber in the grass across the road, chasing a bird or a bug, looking exactly like what he was: an oversized yellow tom.

She smiled at the sight and thought of something her granddaughter, Nancy, had said to her the day before. "Good God, Grandma, but you spoil that cat of yours more than you did any one of us."

Helen chuckled, deciding the girl was probably right. But then, she had plenty of time to dote on Amber, what with Joe gone and her living by herself.

Plenty of time.

Uh-oh.

She held her watch near enough to read its face without putting on her glasses. She grimaced at the placement of the hands. "Hurry up," she prodded, "or you'll be late."

She hopped off the wicker sofa, grabbing up her purse and hurrying out the door without bothering to lock up. She'd very nearly forgotten what day it was and fairly flew the several blocks to the beauty shop.

Helen arrived at LaVyrle's Cut 'n' Curl for her appointment with but a minute to spare. LaVyrle Hunnecker, operator and proprietress, was big on punctuality. "Would you show up late for one of Bertha Beaner's teas?" Helen had once heard LaVyrle chastise a tardy client, a dark brow lifted beneath her teased web of blond hair. "Or for a physical with Doc Melville?" She'd harrumphed, and the red-cheeked late arrival had sighed in agreement.

The ladies who patronized the place knew good and well how LaVyrle, a strong woman despite her slight stature, could make their half-hour appointment one of misery, dismissing the shampoo girl and using her own steady fingers to tug and pull and wring one's head with a roughness that left the scalp tingling for a good forty-eight hours after. And Helen, no namby-pamby herself—she couldn't afford to be at seventy-five and a grandmother of nine—didn't savor the thought of one of LaVyrle's vindictive washes today.

She gave a self-conscious pat to her wiry gray hair as she pushed the door open and walked inside. The smell of hairspray and flower-scented shampoo assailed her as she gave the ponytailed receptionist-cum-shampoo-girl a sheepish grin. She hurried past a row of occupied helmet hair dryers and slipped into a chair within eyeshot of the cubicle where LaVyrle worked her magic.

"Good afternoon, everyone," she said and glanced at the mirrored reflection of LaVyrle, who was giving a final blast of hairspray to the neatly coiffed head of the sheriff's wife, Sarah Biddle.

LaVyrle grunted and glanced at her wristwatch before muttering, "You know the routine, Mrs. E. Mary will wash up your hair in a sec. I'm done with Mrs. B here. Just have to ring her up at the desk."

"Well, don't hurry on account of me."

LaVyrle brushed at the purple cape draped about Sarah Biddle's shoulders, unsnapping it and removing it in one quick flick. Then she disappeared from her station with a *rat-a-tat-tat* of high heels; a moment after, Helen heard her giving instructions to Mary in a no-nonsense manner.

"You look lovely, Sarah," Helen said as the sheriff's wife craned her neck this way and that to admire her hair in the mirror.

"LaVyrle always does seem to know what suits a person best," Sarah replied with a satisfied tone.

"I think she must have a sixth sense about her customers," Helen remarked and set her purse beneath the drawer-lined countertop cluttered with brushes, combs, clips, and curlers, not to mention several bottles of mousse, spritz, and sprays.

A hand grabbed at her, fingers plucking at her warm-up jacket, and Helen straightened to meet Sarah's buck-toothed face.

"We were just talking, LaVyrle and I, when you came in. . . ."

"Oh?" Helen dared to ask. "About what?"

"Mattie Oldbridge, of course," Sarah said in a rush, "and how she got robbed the other day while she was in St. Louis with her nephew."

Though Helen had indeed heard about the incident from Mattie herself, she feigned ignorance so as not to deprive Sarah of the fun of telling the story again.

"Frankie—I mean, the sheriff—he thinks it might've been some kids from Green Valley. You know how they like to get drunk and raise a little hell on the weekends. Or it could've been that awful Charlie Bryan. That kid's always up to his ears in trouble."

"You don't say?"

Sarah sucked in her breath. "It's the third burglary in the last couple of months, can you believe? Anyway, Frank thinks they're pawning the stuff they steal, using the money to buy drugs."

Helen sighed. "For goodness' sake."

Sarah scratched at her long chin. "Frank thinks they must've climbed through an open window at Mattie's, because there was no sign of forced entry. In fact, he said the house was closed up as tight as a drum." She paused, head cocked. "He figures the window lock must've accidentally jarred shut when they left." She shrugged. "And they're not taking big things, like TVs or computers, which is strange. It's like they know exactly what they want, get their hands on it, and leave the same way they came."

"Any leads?"

"Not a one," Sarah admitted. "He didn't find a single fingerprint at Mattie's house, well, except for Mattie's. It was the same with the others." Her eyes returned to her mirrored self, and she fussed with the sweep of hair over her ears. "Who knows, maybe they were smart enough to wear gloves or wiped off what they touched. Anything's possible these days."

Helen sighed. "The times are certainly changing, aren't they? It hardly seems so long ago that locks were out of the ordinary here instead of commonplace."

"It's all the drugs," Sarah said, retrieving her bag from beneath LaVyrle's countertop. "Frankie says crimes all over have skyrocketed because of people buying crock."

Helen stifled a grin. "You mean crack?"

"Crock, crack." The sheriff's wife wiggled her fingers. "Whatever it's called, it's taking this country to hell in a hand basket." She dug inside her purse and withdrew a pair of bills, leaving them lying atop LaVyrle's station. With a snap, she shut her bag, and her chin jerked up. "Well, I've got some shopping to do." With a final glance at the mirror and a pat to her hair, she flashed Helen a buck-toothed grin. "See you later."

"Good-bye, dear."

A head popped around the corner and a timid voice squeaked out, "Missus Evans? If you're ready, I'll shampoo you now."

"Of course, Mary."

"And don't forget to give Mrs. E a nice long conditioning," LaVyrle's sturdy tone reminded as she grabbed the broom and swept out her cubby. "We can't have her leaving here with her hair looking as dry as a straw."

"Flattery will get you nowhere, LaVyrle," Helen quipped over her shoulder as she followed the girl to the shampoo room.

As Mary worked the soap into Helen's scalp with nimble fingers, Helen closed her eyes. She thought of Sarah Biddle's remarks about Mattie Oldbridge being robbed, of there being several other such thefts in River Bend in recent months, ones the sheriff attributed to boys from the valley searching for things to pawn to get money for drugs; and she wondered what the world was coming to when a town of two hundred or so, snugly set between the river bluffs, miles away from the big city, wasn't even safe enough.

Chapter 2

SHERIFF FRANK BIDDLE headed over to the Bryan house in his dusty cruiser and parked as close to the place as he could get, which wasn't all that near.

Tucked against the bluff to one side of River Bend's tiny harbor, the Bryans' address had no such convenience as a driveway. Frank left the car in the harbor lot, which consisted of gravel ringed by railroad ties. He walked across grass and mud, past the docks, where a dozen small boats bobbed against the ropes binding them. The opaque brown of the Mississippi water that flowed into the inlet gently slapped the muddy banks.

The fishy odor of the river invaded his nostrils, and Frank found himself holding his breath. He got across the wooden bridge that led onto the Bryans' property before he exhaled again. He should have been used to the smell of it by now. He'd been working in this cozy town on the Mississippi for more years than he cared to count.

But then, Frank had seen even longtime River Bend residents pinch their noses when they got too near the water.

The grass grew high on the other side of the bridge. When he stepped into it, the blades came up past his trouser cuffs. Weeds poked their way through a cracked concrete path snaking up to the house. For all its neglect, the place looked peaceful enough sitting in the shade of the trees. Its foundation was notched into the side of the bluff so it almost seemed a part of the rocks behind it.

As he approached the door, Frank realized the white-washed exterior looked about as ragged as the craggy bluffs themselves. The paint peeled in long strips; the yellow of the trim had flaked away almost entirely in spots.

He shook his head.

Ray Bryan, at eighty-some-odd, was simply not fit enough anymore to keep up the house, and he had no spare funds to hire someone else to do it. He did have Charlie, his grandson, living with him, but the kid was no help. All he seemed to do was make trouble for the old man.

In fact, Charlie was the reason Biddle had come.

He knocked on the door, trying to peer through the gritty panes of glass.

"Ray? Charlie? Hey, anyone home?"

The door came open slowly. A suspicious brown eye peered out. "Sheriff Biddle? Yeesh." The door cracked wider, and the disgruntled face of a boy stared at him. "Can you keep it down? My grandpop's sleeping."

"I need to talk to you, Charlie. So either you step outside, or I'll have to ask you to let me in."

"All right already." The boy slipped out and quietly shut the door behind him. He plunked down on the front porch step. He had the hood of his sweatshirt pulled over his head, and his dark jeans had about as many holes as his sneakers. "What's it this time, huh? And can you make it quick? I got a lot of things to do."

Frank descended the stoop and stood on the broken walk, facing Charlie. "You got anything you want to confess?"

"Confess? What are you now, a priest?" The boy pushed his hoodie off and ran a hand over his stubble of hair.

Biddle wondered if Charlie had done the crew cut himself. The close-clip added further menace to the boy's permanently scowling features. "I'm only trying to cut you some slack."

"Yeah, right." Charlie rolled his eyes.

"You remember what I came 'round to see you about last month and the month before that?"

"Like I could forget." Charlie started picking at the dirt beneath his fingernails. "A few rich old biddies had stuff stolen from their houses, and you thought I had something to do with it." Charlie glared at Biddle from beneath the thick slant of his eyebrows.

Biddle sighed. "I didn't accuse you, son. I merely asked if you might've been involved or if you knew who pulled it off."

"I'm always the first one you blame, aren't I?" Charlie scuffed the heel of his sneaker against the ground.

"Well, you have gotten yourself in enough messes before."

"Hey, I'm sixteen. I'm supposed to rebel."

Biddle lifted a hand and began counting off on his fingers. "Twice you've been caught skinny-dipping in the community pool drunk as a skunk—"

"So maybe I was hot and thirsty."

"You broke into the mayor's car—"

Charlie grunted. "That piece of junk? I was just seeing if it would actually run."

Biddle put a foot up on the first step and leaned forward, looking Charlie right in the eye, but the kid just turned his head. "I asked you before if you were the one who broke into Mavis White's and Violet Farley's—"

"And I told you I didn't!" Charlie's nostrils flared.

"I'm asking you now if you hit Mattie Oldbridge's house while she was out of town."

"And I'm telling you again that I didn't do it!" Charlie jumped to his feet, face flushed and hands balled into fists.

"You have an alibi?" Biddle stared at the small, wiry kid poised to fight. Why did short guys always seem to have such big chips on their shoulders?

"Why do I need an alibi?" Charlie scoffed. "I know I'm no Goody Two-shoes, but I didn't bust into any of those old ladies' houses, okay? So get off my back!"

He glowered at Biddle before he stomped up the steps and disappeared inside.

Biddle didn't move for a moment. He stood and stared ahead at the paint-peeled façade and then up at the gray spiderwebs that crisscrossed the eaves. "Well, okay then," he said to himself before he turned around and walked away.

Charlie might have denied committing the burglaries, but Frank wasn't sure whether or not to believe him. The kid could lie with the best of them. He'd done it before, and the sheriff didn't doubt he'd do it again at every chance.

Chapter 3

"PERFECT," GRACE SIMPSON said, her head bobbing as she finished reading through the final chapter of her freshly printed manuscript. She tapped the bottom edge neatly against her desk to straighten all the pages.

"Absolutely perfect," she murmured as she slipped the unpublished tome into an expandable file and secured the elastic band around it. She picked up the black flash drive from her blotter and palmed it for a moment. It held the only electronic file of the document, so far as Grace was aware. She didn't trust technology any more than she trusted people. Both seemed destined to betray her, which is why she'd written her opus in longhand on a series of legal pads and had had her assistant transcribe it. She'd forbidden Nancy to save the file to a hard drive, and she'd refused to email the book to the university press that was set to publish it. Grace was too afraid of getting hacked.

Call her paranoid, but in this day and age, she figured paranoid meant safe. With a satisfied sigh, she deposited the flash drive in her top desk drawer and locked it up. Then she picked up a pencil and tapped it against her chin, a smile working its way onto her thin lips.

"Just wait till they get their grubby little mitts on this!" she said out loud. "It's more than they bargained for, that's for sure. My God, but that stuffed-shirt Harold Faulkner and his staff of spiritual do-gooders at the university press are going to see dollar signs through their pompous-colored glasses. They thought this was just going to be another boring study of therapy in a small town. Ha! It'll make all those studies by Masters and Johnson look like kid stuff."

Grace leaned back against her leather chair, shifting comfortably within its oiled folds. She closed her eyes and imagined the impact her book was going to have on the field of psychotherapy. Forget psychotherapy! This thing would be an out-and-out best seller.

Relationships were hot. Sex was a surefire draw. Pain was icing on the cake, and perversion, even better.

Grace felt a chill race up her spine and ran the pencil's eraser across her bottom lip, thinking that right there—right in that brown cardboard file—she had the precise amount of each ingredient, enough to put her where she wanted to be: not only on top of her profession but on top of the world, where she belonged.

"On our program today, we have the renowned therapist and author Grace Simpson, here to talk about her book *Small Town Secrets: Therapy Outside the Big City. . . .*"

She could already hear Oprah announcing her, and she pictured herself seated upon one of those cushy chairs on set, the bright lights shining down and the live audience clapping. Grace blushed as she envisioned the applause growing increasingly loud. No doubt she'd shine so brightly that Oprah would give her a show of her own, like that scrub-wearing Dr. Oz.

"Grace, can we talk?"

Yes, Oprah? she nearly said. But then she opened her eyes to see the figure standing tentatively inside the door to her office, and her grin quickly turned upside-down.

"Nancy?" A wave of cold washed out Grace's momentary flush of imagined glory. She wrinkled her brow and stared at her assistant. "I thought you'd already gone."

The young woman nervously pushed mousy brown hair behind her ears. "You said you wanted that report for the Psychotherapy Society typed up and ready by morning, and you didn't give it to me until after lunch. Plus, I had to go over to your place to meet with the dishwasher repairman at three o'clock, and then I had to print a copy of your book—"

"Stop," Grace said, cutting off Nancy's long-winded excuse for lurking about the office after six. "Whining doesn't become you. If the job's too much for you, then maybe you're not the person I thought you were."

"No." Nancy's porcelain features whitened further. "That's not what I was getting at." She gestured helplessly, seeming unable to find the words. "You said I could talk to you any time, and I think that time is now."

"What's the problem?" Grace asked and tossed the pencil down. "Don't tell me you want overtime because you can't get everything done during normal business hours."

"You do give me an awful lot to type," the girl groused.

"You know I hate computers, Nancy. As I explained when I hired you, I write all my notes by hand. It's imperative that my assistant transcribe everything from session notes to this"—she set a hand possessively atop the pleated folder that held her manuscript.

"Of course, I knew that." Nancy looked like she was about to cry. "It's not just about my workload. It's about how you treat me."

"You feel unappreciated, is that it? I don't pat you on the head enough? Would you like me to stick gold stars on your task list?"

Nancy lifted her chin, but it trembled nonetheless. "Please, Grace, don't do this. I'm not a child."

"Well, right now you're acting like a child who doesn't know when it's time to go home. So, please, leave." Grace stood up but kept her hand on her manuscript. "And don't forget that you're not to say a word about anything you read while you were typing my book. If you do"— Grace paused, her chest tightening—"I will make sure you regret it."

"Of course I won't."

"You did destroy my notes?" Grace interrupted. "You put all handwritten pages through the cross-shredder?"

"That's what you asked me to do, wasn't it?" Nancy replied, sounding affronted.

"So I have the only hard copy right here?" Grace nodded at the item centered on her desk. "And there are no other e-files but the one on the flash drive?"

Nancy's eyes flashed. "Don't you trust me?"

No, Grace wanted to respond. She didn't trust a soul, and with good reason.

"Just go home," Grace snapped. "I have a lot on my mind, and I need to be alone."

Nancy uttered a final, reluctant, "But, Grace, we need to—"

"Goodnight, Nancy," Grace cut her off again.

With a look of resignation, the slender figure retreated. Grace held her breath for a moment after, straining to hear the telltale noise of the door onto Main Street open and shut. She breathed out again.

Good. The girl was gone.

Grace shook her head. Fresh out of college, armed with an undergrad degree in psychology, and they thought they should be allowed to do more than just push papers and answer the phone.

Hah!

It had taken Grace nearly thirty-three years to get where she was, years of research and study, of attending innumerable boring lectures and symposiums, of slaving away pro bono doing social work and playing second fiddle to half a dozen more renowned therapists in St. Louis and thereabouts, finally going off on her own, only to find her practice full of the low-pay or no-pay cases her colleagues rejected, her peers snubbing her all the while. Max had been the one to suggest getting out of the city entirely. Yes, it had been her dear husband's idea to try her luck in a town outside St. Louis that wasn't already overflowing with enough psychs to populate a small country. It was only after she'd taken the plunge and set up her practice in picturesque River Bend that she'd understood darling Max's reasons for wanting her out of the city: he'd been sleeping with one of the salesgirls at his sporting goods store. Grace had confronted him about the affair, and Max hadn't even denied it. She'd kicked him out pronto, she recalled, though the memory of it was less than fond.

She shifted in her chair and sniffled.

Max had popped into River Bend once or twice since their separation, acting forlorn and trying to woo her back, but Grace had fought the stubborn feelings that remained. Grace Simpson was nobody's patsy. She had no intentions of delaying the divorce any longer. God knows, she'd never take him back, especially not now, when she had her future by the balls. Max would just have to keep banging his salesgirls and muddling along without her.

Grace sighed and fixed her eyes on the manuscript again.

Well, she did have one reason to be grateful to her almost-ex-hubby. River Bend had turned out to be more of a gold mine than she'd ever imagined. The tiny town was chockfull of well-heeled widows and retirees, their plump nest eggs ripe for the picking. And that didn't include the towns around it, like Jerseyville, big enough to have a country club, a main drag lined with fast-food joints, and the ever-present Walmart; Alton, far more populated still, with enough car dealerships to make Detroit proud; and cozy Grafton up the road, with its adorable winery, restaurants, and bluff homes with river views. Grace had handed her cards out right and left, at hospitals and nursing homes, at bingo games and bridge tournaments, until she'd reeled in enough messed-up lives to fill her practice to the hilt.

Even still, she wasn't taken seriously by her big-city colleagues. River Bend might be picturesque, but it was in the boonies, nonetheless. Her clients were practically Hoosiers, for want of a better description.

Grace let out a loud snort.

The very first thing she'd do when her book was published and the recognition started pouring in was set up an office somewhere else, like Chicago or, better still, New York.

Ah, yes, Manhattan, Grace mused with a self-satisfied smile. Now, that was a place full of bona fide loony tunes, enough to provide juicy revelations for not just one measly book but a flipping encyclopedia!

Then everyone would know what Grace Simpson was made of. The professional journals that kept turning down her articles, the leaders of the conferences that kept declining her offers to speak, the snooty members of the Psychotherapy Society who considered her a failure: she'd show them all, wouldn't she?

Grace picked up the expandable envelope containing her manuscript and hugged it as if it were a life raft, which, in a way, it was.

Chapter 4

HELEN DUCKED OUT of LaVyrle's Cut 'n' Curl and took a slow drag of fresh air, her lungs so full of hairspray that she felt buzzed. She bent her head to tuck her wallet into her purse and didn't see the woman coming at her down the sidewalk—not until their arms bumped, jostling Helen so that she dropped her handbag to her feet, scattering its contents.

The woman let out a surprised "oh," as a large tote bag fell from her arms, spilling out a host of legal pads, which sprawled across the sidewalk, yellow pages fluttering in the breeze.

"I'm so sorry," they both said at once, "I didn't see you!"

As Helen stooped to recover her pocketbook, the other woman crouched to help, and Helen realized she was looking into the tousled hair and flushed face of her granddaughter.

"Helen, Nancy? Everything all right?" a voice boomed from nearby as Bertha Beaner ambled up. "Oh, my, let me help," she offered and set down her own oversized bag to collect the scattered legal pads Nancy had dropped.

Nancy seemed to panic, snatching yellow pages from Bertha's hands. "I've got it, thank you, Mrs. Beaner," she insisted, scrambling to shove the papers back into her tote.

"If you say so," Bertha said and turned her back for a moment to collect her handbag. "I need to hustle anyway," the woman said to Helen and jerked her head toward the salon. "I've got a date with LaVyrle."

Helen replied, "No, don't be late," but she wasn't worried about Bertha getting one of LaVyrle's lectures once she disappeared inside. She was worried about Nancy. Something was wrong.

"Sweetie," she asked and touched the young woman's arm. "What's got you in such a hurry? Have you finally decided to run away from your job with Grace Simpson?"

If she expected to elicit a smile from her granddaughter, she failed miserably.

Instead, Nancy cast a worried eye up the street and quickly shushed her. "Grace has ears like a bat," she said under her breath, "except when I need to talk about my position."

"So you didn't get the chance to chat with her?" Helen knew that Nancy had been summoning up the courage to do so for the past week.

Nancy shook her head. "She basically ordered me to scram."

Helen made a sympathetic cluck.

"Maybe I should go back to school and get my master's sooner instead of later," her granddaughter suggested. "I thought real-world experience would be a plus, but working for Grace is more pain than gain."

"I'm sorry, sweetheart," Helen said helplessly. "Like your grandpa used to tell me every time life disappointed me, all is not lost. When things don't work out, it means there's something better out there."

And Helen was sure that was true in this case.

It wasn't long after Nancy had taken the job with Grace straight out of college that Helen had realized assisting the town's only psychotherapist wasn't easy. Nancy often grumbled about Grace's fear of computers and inability to type, much less do any administrative work for herself. *I have to buy office supplies on my dime, Grandma,* Nancy had told her, *and she doesn't reimburse me for a month.*

Nancy sighed with frustration. "I thought I'd be gaining insight into the profession, but instead I'm just a glorified toady."

"If Grace is so unbearable, maybe you *should* quit," Helen said firmly.

Nancy opened her mouth to respond but ended up shaking her head. "I'm not a quitter, and you know it. Besides, she might treat me like her minion, but she really cares about the profession. She's interested in why people do the things they do, and she honestly wants to help them."

"Honestly?" Helen repeated and arched her eyebrows. "She sure doesn't seem to want to help *you,* seeing how she's always having you run her errands and wait for repairmen." Her granddaughter's duties seemed to cover everything from chauffer to lackey to laundry picker-upper. "That hardly sounds like a position with room for advancement."

"Yeah, I thought I'd learn more about the field than about how to make really good coffee. And, yes, there are times I want to wring Grace's neck," Nancy said, holding tight to the tote bag and patting it. "But if this book does for Grace what I think it will, it could be a break-through for me as well. Being her assistant could really mean something then."

"And you're willing to wait and see?"

Nancy bit her lip. "I guess I am."

Helen wasn't sure why River Bend needed a therapist in the first place. After all, they had the resident pastor who presided over their nondenominational chapel and never ignored a plea for help. Although, Helen admitted to herself, they did seem to go through resident pastors like Kleenex. Their last preacher, Dr. Fister, had remained for only a year, and the church had scrambled to find a re-placement. They had Doc Melville for medical issues and LaVyrle Hunnecker at the beauty shop for anything else. Any additional set of ears—and costly ones at that, from what Nancy had mentioned—seemed above and beyond the necessary.

Despite Helen's misgivings, Grace Simpson had ap-peared to do quite well. The novelty of it had certainly drawn her clientele initially. "According to my therapist" seemed to be the anthem of the twenty-first century, even in a town as small as this.

Ah, progress, Helen mused, and her stomach rumbled.

"Are you hungry?" she asked, wondering if Nancy had dinner plans, though the girl was always so busy with work that Helen doubted it. "Nancy?"

But the young woman didn't seem to hear. She was digging deep inside her tote, a worried frown on her face. She started looking around on the sidewalk.

"Are you all right?" Helen asked.

Nancy bit her lower lip. "Grace was being so awful, and I left in such a hurry, that I must've forgotten one of the legal pads in my desk."

"Do you need to go back?" Helen asked. "Are they important?"

"Yes, they're important, and no, I don't want to go back." Nancy shuddered. "I'm not in the mood for another tongue-lashing, and I wouldn't want Grace to find out that I haven't shredded these yet." She patted the leather tote. "They're the handwritten notes for Grace's book that I finished transcribing this morning. I was supposed to have cross-shredded everything already, but I haven't had time. If she knew I still had them—" Nancy paused and drew a finger across her throat.

"Aw, you poor, mistreated creature," Helen teased and put an arm around the girl. "How about I buy you dinner? We're not going to run into Attila the Therapist at the diner, are we?"

"No, Grace won't be eating at the diner tonight," Nancy said and looked behind her. "But we'd better get a move on or we might bump into her here on the sidewalk. Grace has a six-thirty appointment with LaVyrle and then a dinner meeting in St. Louis with her publisher. She wouldn't let me email the book, can you believe? She wants to hand over the sole hard copy to Harold Faulkner in person."

"Luddite," Helen muttered, although she was enough of one herself. She preferred her old landline to the "smart" phone that Patsy, her eldest daughter and Nancy's mother, had given her last Christmas. Maybe the phone was smart, but all its confusing bells and whistles made Helen feel pretty dumb.

"Not so much a Luddite as paranoid," Nancy said, shifting her tote bag so she could take her grandmother's hand. With a final glance back, she tugged Helen along, walking so quickly that Helen felt out of breath by the time they'd reached the Main Street Diner.

When they'd been seated in a booth and the waitress had brought them water and menus, Helen dared to ask, "So what do you think of the book? You're the only one who's seen it besides Grace, I presume."

"Eh," Nancy said, burying her nose in the menu.

"Don't give me that," Helen whispered, leaning forward. "You must have an opinion. Everyone in town's already speculating about it."

"No kidding." Nancy sighed and put the menu down. "I've already fielded dozens of calls about Grace's manuscript. It got so bad today that I started letting them all go to voice mail. I don't know why Grace is so worried about who sees the thing beforehand, when she's been dropping hints about it all over River Bend, ticking people off for weeks." Nancy set her elbows on the table and plunked her chin into her hands. "Now everyone who's ever been in for a session is afraid she's put them in there." Nancy looked over at Helen, her forehead wrinkled. "Despite the fact that Grace used pseudonyms, people are freaked out about being recognized, and I can't blame them. This isn't L.A. It's more like Mayberry."

Helen took a slow sip of water. She'd heard the gossip about Grace's book, of course. The rumor mill ran rampant in River Bend. How could it not, with only two hundred residents and everyone seeming to know each other's business? But talk was one thing. Having your peccadilloes exposed in black and white for the public to see was another thing entirely.

"Is it legal?" Helen finally asked. "Doesn't Grace need permission to write about real people and their problems?"

"She's covered so long as she doesn't use their real names and fudges with their social standings and professions a bit," Nancy said. "Grace checked it out with her publisher's legal department. It's an academic press, so they're strict about rules."

"Otherwise, they'd be sued out of business."

"No doubt." Nancy nodded, and her eyes clouded over.

"You've seen what's on the pages," Helen said, cocking her head. "Do folks have cause to worry?"

Nancy fidgeted. "Okay, so maybe I did wonder a bit if the man with the heavyset wife and impotence problem was Art Beaner and if the woman who felt her authority-figure husband had started wearing ladies' panties because he found her unattractive was Sheriff Biddle's wife, Sarah."

Helen had taken a sip of water, and she had to fight to keep from spitting it out all over the table.

"But who am I to say?" Nancy went on with a shrug. "I don't know anyone in town as well as you do, Grandma." She reached across the table to give Helen's hand a squeeze. "How about we forget about Grace and her stupid book and order some dinner? I don't know about you, but I'm starved."

Helen smiled thinly.

She was hardly the only citizen of River Bend who knew her neighbors so well that pseudonyms would not be cloak enough. And once the townsfolk got their hands on copies of Grace Simpson's "stupid book," she could only imagine the trouble it was going to cause.

Chapter 5

"I HAVE AN appointment at six-thirty," Grace stated crisply, stepping up to the receptionist's desk. Behind it sat Mary, an impossibly shy creature with a head of lank hair that seemed to forever fall into the girl's eyes, despite her attempt at harnessing the mess of it into a ponytail.

"She isn't running behind, is she?" Grace glanced at the gold watch on her wrist, thinking that she had to leave town by seven-thirty at the latest if she wanted to arrive on time for her eight o'clock meeting with her publisher at Tony's in downtown St. Louis. "I'm on a tight schedule—"

"No," Mary quietly interrupted. "LaVyrle's never late."

"Good."

"She's finishing up with Mrs. Beaner, so if you wouldn't mind having a seat. Um, we've got the latest *Midwest Travelers* magazine in if you'd like to take a peek."

"I'm good." Grace sat down and stared toward the salon's rear where LaVyrle had her private cubby. As she shifted to get comfortable, the chair's vinyl upholstery emitted a series of squeaks.

She found a dog-eared copy of *Good Housekeeping* and was impatiently thumbing through it when she inhaled a strong dose of hairspray from above. She slowly raised her eyes to see Bertha Beaner, the bigger, if not better, half of Art Beaner, chairman of the town board, glaring down at her. She clutched a large satchel to her heaving chest as her beady eyes shot daggers.

"Hello, Bertha," Grace said, bracing herself for what was to come. "Can I help you with something?"

"Help? That's the last thing I'd want from you!" the woman said with a snort. "I do hope you're satisfied with yourself, Grace Simpson. "You've got this whole town all shook up."

Grace set aside the magazine and calmly asked, "What exactly are you accusing me of?"

"You must know I mean your horrid book!"

"Ah, my horrid book." Grace wrinkled her brow, setting her hands in her lap. It was hardly the first time one of River Bend's denizens had approached her lately and acted as if she were Lucifer. Funny, because not too long before that, they had behaved as though she were a savior, there to solve all their problems. "I find it interesting how excitable everyone's gotten when it's not even published. How can you judge a book you haven't even read?"

Something changed in Bertha's doughy face, and she reached inside her satchel, withdrawing a legal-sized pad full of rumpled yellow pages. "Oh, I've read enough."

Grace blinked. No, she told herself. It couldn't be. Nancy had kept everything under lock and key while she'd typed up the book. And she'd looked Grace in the eye not twenty minutes ago, assuring her that the notes had been destroyed.

"Cat got your tongue?" Bertha snapped, and her over-ripe features flushed. She leaned in to hiss, "How dare you ask us to trust you with our deepest secrets, only to peddle them to a publisher for profit! And you have the nerve to call it academic! Rubbish!" Mrs. Beaner puffed. "It's disgusting, that's what it is, Grace Simpson, and if you go through with this publishing deal, either God will strike you down for it, or one of us will!"

"How did you get that?" Grace grunted and jumped from her chair, snatching the yellow pages from Bertha's grip. "It belongs to me!"

Bertha looked mad enough to spit. Instead, she turned on her heel and slapped a bill on the counter in front of a wide-eyed Mary. Then she stomped out of the beauty shop with her newly-coiffed head held high. The door shut with a bang, and the plate-glass window behind Grace rattled.

Grace felt rattled as well.

Would all of River Bend blame her for the broken water main last winter, too? How about the murder that happened before she'd even moved to town?

"So she's a fan of yours, huh?"

Grace hadn't noticed LaVyrle approach. She'd been too busy wondering if she should fire Nancy tonight or wait until her incompetent assistant showed up at work in the morning.

"Yeah, my biggest fan," Grace muttered, trying not to tremble as she bent the legal pad in half and stuffed it inside her purse.

"People are funny." LaVyrle's dark brows arched high above eyelids painted a robin's egg blue. "They sure like talkin' about others, but they don't like it a bit when they hear someone talkin' about them."

Grace rose from her seat, taking a step toward the beautician. "Ah, LaVyrle," she said and set her hand on the woman's shoulder. "I do believe you're the only person in town who knows more about the people who live here than I do."

"Right," LaVyrle remarked as she led the way toward her secluded station. "But with you, all they get for their money is advice. With me, they get an ear to listen, plus a cut and blow-dry."

Grace couldn't help but smile. "And that's why therapists will never put hair salons out of business."

"You got that right, Mrs. S," LaVyrle replied, chuckling. "Just leave your purse under the counter and head on back so Mary can shampoo you."

"Yes, yes, I know the routine by heart," Grace said and ditched her bag as instructed. It wasn't as though Bertha Beaner was going to stomp back to LaVyrle's and try to steal the legal pad. She'd already seen enough to get her good and riled.

"I'll get you all fixed up for that dinner in St. Louis I heard you tellin' Mary about," the beautician assured her.

"You're a godsend, LaVyrle."

"Me?" LaVyrle blushed. "Nah," she said with a flip of her hand. "I'm just a girl doing her best to make an honest buck."

Grace grinned at LaVyrle, thinking she probably liked the small-town beautician better than anyone else in this burg. LaVyrle reminded her of a kindhearted and middle-aged gangster's moll. "What I think, sweetie," Grace said as she headed off to the shampoo sink around the corner, "is that there's a lot more to you than anyone knows."

"That's 'cause I do all of the listening and they do all the yakkin'," LaVyrle hollered after her.

And it was a good thing they did talk, Grace mused as she tracked down Mary for a shampoo, or else there would've been nothing for her to write about and less still about which the patrons of LaVyrle's could gossip.

Chapter 6

HELEN HATED THAT Nancy couldn't even relax and enjoy her dinner. The girl only ordered soup and barely ate more than a few spoonfuls. She mostly spent her time looking worried and fiddling with the saltines until they'd dissolved into crumbs.

At 6:35, the door to the diner jingled open and Bertha Beaner burst in, her cheeks red and eyes blazing fire.

Helen lifted her hand to wave, but Bertha didn't notice. She made a beeline for a table where Sarah Biddle sat with Clara Foley.

"What's wrong, Grandma?" Nancy asked the same question Helen had been posing to her for the past half hour.

"I'm not sure," Helen told her, watching the women bend their heads together, chattering furiously, before they all got up and went to another table filled with women Helen knew from Stitch and Sew and bridge club. "But something is definitely up."

It was then that Bertha looked across the diner and saw Helen and Nancy.

She didn't smile or wave. Instead, she scowled. The rest of the ladies stopped talking and glanced over as well.

"They look downright pissed," Nancy whispered.

Helen thought that was an understatement, and she braced herself as the group of women—now half a dozen strong—stopped at the end of the booth she shared with Nancy.

Bertha set her palms on the table and leaned forward, directing her anger at Helen's granddaughter. "I don't know how you can work for Grace Simpson and hold your head up!"

Nancy visibly flinched.

"Don't bully her, Bertha Beaner," Helen said in her granddaughter's defense. "She's Gracie's assistant, not her keeper."

"Well, I read the filthy notes you dropped," Bertha shouted at Nancy. She slammed down her fist. "And I won't stand for that book getting published. Someone needs to put that awful woman in her place, and that's what we aim to do right now! Come on, girls, Grace Simpson's at LaVyrle's!" she called out like a rallying cry and led her cohorts out the door.

"So that's where it went," Nancy muttered and grabbed her leather bag. She scooted out of the booth, rushing off before Helen could grab a twenty from her purse to toss on the table.

"Nancy, wait!" Helen called as her granddaughter set the bells to jangling on the diner's front door.

Helen didn't have far to go to catch up. Barely a block down Main Street, the crowd had gathered beneath the purple sign for LaVyrle's Cut 'n' Curl.

Nancy had stopped on the outskirts, and Helen did the same.

"Oh, no, this is my fault," Nancy murmured. "Grace is going to kill me for losing those notes."

"How is it your fault?" Helen asked, standing shoulder to shoulder. "You didn't write the damn book. Grace brought this on herself."

Bertha Beaner tried to push through LaVyrle's front door, but a ponytailed Mary stood in the doorway, blocking her path. "Please, just go, or I'll get the sheriff," the girl said, trying her best to keep the agitated throng from pushing its way inside.

The sheriff's office was right next door, Helen mused; she was surprised Frank Biddle hadn't heard the noise and ambled over.

"Bring out Grace Simpson!" someone yelled.

"She used us!"

Helen remembered Nancy saying that Grace had a hair appointment before her dinner engagement in St. Louis. It certainly appeared that she wasn't going to leave LaVyrle's without plowing through an angry mob.

"Please, don't shout!" The squeaky voice belonged to Mary. "Can't we be civil to each other?"

"Grace Simpson doesn't know the meaning of the word *civil*!" Sarah Biddle shouted back and started chanting, "Stop the press! Stop the press!"

Nancy tugged at Helen's sleeve. "Maybe we should go.

If Grace sees me here"—she swallowed—"she's not going to fire me. She's going to kill me."

Before Helen could even respond, Grace appeared in the doorway. Pushing Mary aside, she stepped onto the stoop, draped in one of LaVyrle's lavender capes. Her hair still had butterfly clips holding up chunks that had yet to be dried.

She stuck her hands on her hips. "Shame on you all for behaving like a pack of unruly children! All this shouting is giving me a headache." Grace waved them away. "Just go on home, why don't you. Go on home, you bunch of overaged crybabies."

Bertha was the first to step forward. "You're the lowest, Grace Simpson, lower than a cockroach, if you ask me!"

Grace stared her down. "I don't recall that I did."

"You're a liar, that's what you are." Sarah Biddle reared her head next. "Taking what we told you in confidence and putting it in your sordid book for the world to read!"

"I didn't betray you." Grace shook her head. "No real names were used. Your identities will remain anonymous."

"Horse hockey!" Bertha countered. "We won't remain anonymous. Real names don't matter in a town as small as this. Everyone will know regardless. I read those notes of yours, and I saw right through your silly pseudonyms."

"Well, that's your sour grapes," Grace said and touched a hand to her head, poking at the clips. "You've no say in the matter. It's all said and done, and perfectly legal."

"You're evil, Grace Simpson. Pure evil!" one of the women called out. "You're the devil himself!"

Helen glanced around and realized more townsfolk had gathered. It looked like the diner had emptied out. Bodies jostled her on either side, and she noticed Nancy had been pushed forward, closer to where Bertha stood.

"Take this, you witch!" a voice bellowed from down the sidewalk, and a pair of tomatoes zipped through the air toward an unsuspecting Grace. One missed its mark and splattered harmlessly against the plate glass. The other struck Grace full in the chest, splashing red down the lavender bib and leaving a bloody stain.

"Damn you crazy bumpkins!" Grace wailed. "Look what you've done!" Her cheeks flushed. Eyes wild, she scanned the vociferous crowd. "You'll be sorry for this, all of you will! You can't treat me this way after all I've done—"

Abruptly, she stopped.

Helen followed the direction of her stare, which seemed to fix directly upon Nancy.

"You," Grace said, pointing her finger and shaking it. "You're responsible for this! You left my notes lying around for anyone to see!"

"I-I didn't m-mean to," Nancy stammered as Helen tried to wiggle her way forward. "You didn't give me time to shred everything! You had me running your errands and waiting on repairmen instead of doing my job."

"Doing your job?" Grace let out a sour laugh. "As of this moment, you don't have a job, my dear. You're fired!" Then Grace turned on her heel with a flap of lavender cape, disappearing into the shop.

Helen got to her granddaughter and grabbed her

hand. It felt ice-cold. Nancy trembled, tears in her eyes, humiliation written all over her face.

"What in tarnation is going on here?" Sheriff Biddle said, wading into the throng.

Helen wondered what the heck had taken him so long.

"Why, Frankie, we were just expressing our First Amendment right to free speech," Sarah Biddle piped up as Helen tugged Nancy away by the hand.

The crowd grumbled and flung several last epithets after Grace's departed figure before the contingent began to slowly disperse.

"I didn't mean to lose those pages," Nancy was saying. "She didn't even listen."

"I know," Helen told her as they stopped walking. She set her hands on Nancy's shoulders. "Grace should have understood that it was a mistake."

"It's so unfair," Nancy muttered. "After all I've done for her. I've worked day and night to make her happy, and it was never enough." A shudder passed through her slim frame. "I hate her, Grandma, I do," she said, sniffling and wiping her nose with the back of her hand. "I'm so mad, I could choke her."

"Get in line," a familiar voice said, and, as she walked passed them, Bertha Beaner added, "you're hardly the only one who'd like nothing better than to see that woman dead."

Chapter 7

GRACE SQUINTED AT her reflection in her bathroom mirror, scrutinizing her makeup. She decided the pale brown on her eyelids and pale pink on her lips looked just about right, giving her a sparkle of youth despite the ever-present grooves and wrinkles.

She patted her newly done hair, hoping it would settle down a little. The fat brush LaVyrle had used to dry and style her short cut made it poof out more than she was used to, but Grace liked it well enough.

Her dress was a taupe color, nothing fancy. A simple sheath with long sleeves, shoes to match. It was tasteful and elegant, the perfect attire for a soon-to-be best-selling author.

"You're on your way up, Grace Simpson," she said aloud as she admired herself, giving in to a smile.

She was but a pinch away, all right. Tonight she would hand over the only copy of her manuscript to her publisher.

So what if that pretentious Harold Faulkner wasn't thrilled that she wouldn't just email him the file? He'd whined about having to scan the thing before he could even begin to edit, but Grace figured that wasn't her problem. "Do you want the book or not?" she'd asked him, and he'd given in after muttering something about "eccentric authors."

But Grace didn't care.

Stepping over to her dressing table, she picked up the purple bottle of Christian Dior's Poison that she'd bought herself last Christmas and had hardly used, finding no occasion special enough to merit smelling that good.

But this evening was different.

She gently eased out the stopper and rolled it once beneath her nose. "Delicious," she whispered. Lifting her left arm, she shook back her silk sleeve then touched the scent to her wrist. It was then, when she'd turned her wrist slightly around, that she caught sight of her watch. Its hands pointed precisely to 7:35.

"Good God!" she exhaled, realizing then she'd never make it into St. Louis and to her meeting on time if she didn't leave pronto and drive like a bat out of hell. Grace had always been a prompt woman, had always expected others to be likewise, and she wasn't about to screw up tonight of all nights.

With a clatter, she set the perfume bottle down and ran about the bedroom, prodding piles of discarded clothing in search of her matching taupe handbag. When she finally retrieved it from beneath a rumpled blouse, she went in hot pursuit of her keys, finding them downstairs on the kitchen counter.

She locked the front door in haste. Her heels clacked upon the whitewashed steps as she rushed down from the porch to her car. She was off in a shot, ignoring the stare of her neighbor, Mattie Oldbridge, who was sitting on her front stoop with a beer in her hand, dressed like a bag lady to boot.

"Despite all her money," Grace murmured.

As she pulled away from the curb in a squeal of tires, Grace suddenly remembered that Mattie had been robbed the weekend before, though she found it hard to summon much sympathy. Why should she? She was amply paid for her sympathy by her clients, and Mattie Oldbridge wasn't one of them.

"The old fool probably didn't lock her doors," Grace spoke aloud as she drove out of town and onto the River Road that would take her toward Alton and then across the Mississippi to St. Louis.

What had been stolen, anyhow? She tried to recall what she'd heard. Some money, wasn't it, and pieces of jewelry, plus a few silly candlesticks? Nothing, Grace decided, worth getting one's panties in a wad.

Hugging the wheel, Grace sped along the highway. She looked straight ahead as she went, glancing neither to the right at the brown of the river, nor to her left at the green of the bluffs that hovered protectively over the road.

Twenty minutes from Chautauqua, she came into downtown Alton. She was only vaguely aware of the places she passed: the old buildings, many still standing after a century or more, most closed up and neglected; others turned into a row of antique stores, fronted by flower-filled barrels.

Dress.

Hose.

Shoes.

Perfume.

Grace went through a mental list of her preparations for dinner, wishing she didn't have a sudden niggling sense that she'd forgotten something vital.

Had she brought her purse? It wasn't on the front seat.

She stopped at the light just before the intersection for the bridge. Her foot on the brake, she turned her head to look behind her. Yes. She sighed. There it was on the backseat.

The light went green above her.

She shifted her foot to the gas just as a thought struck her.

"Damn it all!"

She jerked to a stop, earning herself a loud honk from the car right behind her.

Veering away from the right turn lane, she surged ahead. At the corner, she turned the car and went around the block, heading back to the river road.

"You absentminded dolt!" she bellowed, her cheeks warming to red. "How could you have forgotten the manuscript?"

She slapped her palm against the steering wheel and pressed her foot harder on the gas pedal. "Birdbrain," she grumbled, her heartbeat climbing with the rise of her speedometer. She fumed as she realized she'd be late to her meeting. Very late.

She was still furious when she reached River Bend and pulled into her driveway, parking in back by the kitchen door instead of out front, as was her custom. She raced around the car's hood in the dim of twilight. Keys in hand, she climbed the back stoop and reached for the brass knob.

The door came open at her touch.

"Did I forget to lock up?" she mumbled and blamed the stress she was under. She had more than her share, what with Max and the book and that whining Nancy.

With a snort, she pushed her way into the house. She headed through the darkened kitchen, up the hallway, and into the living room, walking right up to the English writing desk in which she'd locked her manuscript.

She retrieved the skeleton key from atop the secretary and opened up the desk. She was reaching for the cardboard file when she heard a sound.

She lifted her head.

There it was again!

Above her head, the floorboards creaked.

Good God, were those footsteps?

Had the thieves who'd gotten into Mattie's house come to prey upon her as well? Grace wondered. Her pulse pumped in her ears as anxiety attacked. Were the culprits just kids from Green Valley, as the sheriff seemed to surmise, or were they hardened criminals who delighted in burgling the homes of single females?

Grace thought of calling Frank Biddle, but her cell was in her purse in the car. Holding the manuscript against her like a shield, she moved quietly toward the stairs, tiptoeing upward.

Pull yourself together, she ordered, heart thumping in her breast. River Bend was hardly a hotbed of crime. Gangs didn't roam about with guns or knives. If it was just some wild-eyed teenager wanting money for drugs, well, she'd give him a twenty to appease him until she could get the sheriff on the phone.

More likely, she realized, it was Bertha Beaner or the sheriff's wife, breaking in while they assumed she was away, searching the house for the manuscript so they could burn it and celebrate.

"Who's there?" she called out, softly at first, and then with more command. "Who's there, I said? If you don't leave right away, I'll have the sheriff here in a minute flat."

A drawer slapped shut.

Was the thief in her bedroom?

Grace felt suddenly spitting mad. "Come out this instant! Make yourself known, you coward." When silence answered, she added, "All right then, I'm coming in!"

At that, she swept into her room, still gripping her manuscript. Two steps inside, she hesitated. In the bureau mirror dead ahead, she caught the reflection of the intruder hiding in the shadow of the half-opened door through which Grace had just entered.

"You?" she got out, staring into the mirror. "What in the world do you think you're do—"

She never had the chance to turn around as something heavy came crashing down on her head, knocking her to the floor, permanently out of breath.

Chapter 8

THE NEXT MORNING, Nancy Sweet got into the shower, dried her hair, and dressed as she always did. She hadn't slept all night. She'd stayed up to shred those stupid notes of Grace's—it was the least she could have done—and hadn't finished until just before seven. Her eyes were puffy from crying and throwing herself a pity party, but she dabbed on concealer and headed to the office, arriving at 7:30, half an hour before Grace, like she always did. Or at least she *had* until Grace had canned her in front of half of River Bend the night before.

Maybe she could reason with Grace, Nancy thought as she unlocked the door to the office. What if she explained what had happened, how the notes had fallen out of her bag on the sidewalk and Bertha Beaner had swiped them? Perhaps then Grace would realize she'd been hasty in firing her, especially after all the extra hours Nancy had put in getting Grace's book notes typed up.

She flipped on the light switch in the waiting room and hesitated. Her gaze roamed the framed Rorschach ink blots upon the walls, and she shook her head.

No, she knew, it would never work. When was the last time Grace had actually listened to her about anything?

The answer was simple: *never*.

Trying to have a rational conversation with Grace at this point was akin to banging her head against the wall.

Nancy sighed and moved into the inner office, passing the coffee machine just as it turned on, its timer set for precisely 7:45.

She might as well pack her things and get out of there. Grace could mail her final paycheck. It would only make things worse if she hung around and bumped into Grace when she arrived at eight o'clock.

Don't cry again, for God's sake, Nancy told herself as tears pricked at the back of her eyelids. She swallowed and focused instead on the tasks at hand.

She went through her desk and grabbed the few things that belonged to her: two framed photographs, the pencil holder made of rolled-up magazine strips one of her nephews had crafted, and a spiral-bound notebook in which she tracked each day's priorities. At least she wouldn't have to worry any more about forgetting a task and setting Grace off, would she?

On impulse, Nancy reached for a blank pad of paper, picked up a pen, and composed a quick note to leave her ex-boss.

"Dear Grace," she wrote in a childish scribble, "You are a hateful, small-minded bitch, and it was hell to come in every day and work for you. I hope your book fails miserably." Then she signed it, "Sincerely, Nancy Sweet."

"Real mature, Nance," she whispered to herself. Her parents would be proud to know that her four years of college had amounted to this. She ripped the page off the pad, wadded it up into a ball, and tossed it into the waste-basket.

No, if she had any last words to say to Grace, she had to do it face-to-face. She'd let the woman run over her for months. Maybe, Nancy figured, it was time she stood up for herself.

Nancy straightened her shoulders.

What did she have to lose? Grace had already fired her.

She made up her mind and decided to stay put, since it was now ten minutes till eight. Grace would arrive soon enough. The woman never strayed from her schedule.

Nancy wandered about the office for a good fifteen minutes, growing impatient as another fifteen ticked past. Grace should have arrived by now, she thought, then felt an uneasy prickle up her spine. She got a bad feeling that had nothing to do with her frustration. What if something had happened to Grace, like she was being held prisoner until she agreed not to publish her book? It didn't seem that far-fetched, especially after the show-down in front of LaVyrle's.

Call it misguided loyalty, but Nancy had to find out if Grace was all right. Once she did, maybe *then* she'd tell her off.

She locked up the office but kept her keys, since one was for Grace's front door. Then she walked the three blocks to the street where Grace lived. She knew the way well enough. She couldn't count the times in weeks past that she'd had to go to Grace's house to wait for the carpenter, the plumber, the painter, the roofer, or the dishwasher repairman. She'd even had to water Grace's plants for a week when her boss had attended a symposium in Austin.

Nancy was so preoccupied with pondering all the ways that Grace had taken advantage of her that she didn't see Mattie Oldbridge standing on the porch next door. She never even heard the woman call out a perky, "Yoo hoo!"

What she did notice was Grace's car, pulled all the way back into her driveway.

So she *was* home.

Nancy sucked in a deep breath and marched up Grace's front steps. Making a fist, she pounded firmly on the door.

"Open up, Grace! It's Nancy," she shouted when she got no response. "I know you're there, so let me in!"

When nothing happened, Nancy stabbed her copy of Grace's house key in the lock, turned the dead bolt, pushed the door wide, and let herself in.

FROM HER PORCH railing, Mattie Oldbridge watched as Nancy Sweet disappeared through Grace Simpson's front door.

The poor child, she thought, seeing how worked up the girl was. The way she'd pounded at the door and yelled for Grace to open up had sent chills up Mattie's spine.

Although seeing Nancy so riled didn't surprise Mattie. She'd heard about Grace firing the girl in front of a crowd at LaVyrle's, so she couldn't blame Nancy for being angry. But Mattie wasn't used to seeing the pretty Miss Sweet so uptight. Usually when Nancy swung by Grace's to do this or that, she was so friendly and kind.

But then Grace Simpson seemed to have a lot of folks worked up these days, didn't she?

A rush of air from off the river ruffled Mattie's hair, but it wasn't just the wind that gave her goose bumps.

She heard the popping of tires on gravel and turned her head to catch Sheriff Biddle's mud-speckled black-and-white coming around the corner. With a squeal of brakes, it stopped in front of Grace's yard.

Oh, no, Mattie thought, hoping Grace hadn't called the sheriff when the girl had let herself into the house. Hadn't Grace caused Nancy embarrassment enough? Would she have the girl arrested, too?

Mattie watched as the sheriff and another man—a distinguished fellow in a dark blue suit—emerged from the squad car and headed up to Grace's front door.

"This is all very odd," Mattie murmured, "very odd indeed."

She pressed herself back into the shadows of the porch and waited.

Just as the sheriff and his companion reached the top of the whitewashed steps, the front door flew wide open and Nancy Sweet raced out the door, clutching something in her hands.

Mattie squinted, wishing she'd thought to put on her

glasses when she'd come out for the paper. What was it Nancy carried? Was it a broom or a stick?

Even without her horned-rims she could see the girl's face was white as bones.

"Whoa now!" the sheriff said and grabbed the girl's arm, forcing her to drop the stick to the ground.

Nancy raised her hands in the air. They appeared muddied to Mattie's unfocused eyes, although the mud around here was brown, not red.

"Help, oh, God, help her, please!" Nancy began to scream so loudly that Mattie felt battered by her voice. "I shouldn't have come. I shouldn't have come," she ranted over and over, and her slim body heaved so that the sheriff had to hold her steady.

The fellow in the dark suit just stood by and gaped.

"She's dead, she's really dead!" Nancy sobbed and slumped against Biddle's chest.

And Mattie did the only thing she possibly could have done after witnessing such a scene: she ran inside, dropped the newspaper, grabbed her phone, and dialed her friend Bertha Beaner.

Chapter 9

"WHAT DO YOU mean you're holding Nancy for questioning?" Helen asked, putting a protective arm around her granddaughter. She glared at Sheriff Biddle across his desk. "You must know that she could no more have killed Grace Simpson than I could."

Biddle sighed, his gaze shifting from the pale face of the girl back to Helen. "Come now, Mrs. Evans. You've got to realize that I'm only doing my job. We found Nancy at the murder scene, holding a bloody bat."

"What you *assume* is the murder scene," Helen replied and tightened her grip on the girl. Nancy had barely uttered a word since Helen had arrived at the sheriff's office, and Helen was worried that her granddaughter had gone into some state of posttraumatic shock.

"Look here," Biddle said and gesticulated wildly, "I'm nearly one hundred percent certain Grace Simpson was killed where we found her. There was no sign she'd been moved, no indication of a struggle or forced entry. Her car was parked outside her kitchen door. Her body was found on her bedroom floor. The blood from her head wounds left stains on the carpet and, of course, the baseball bat that Nancy brought out of the house with her. Doc Melville accompanied the body to the county morgue in Jerseyville. When they've done forensics testing, we'll know more. But until then, Nancy's a person of interest."

Helen pressed her lips together and looked at her granddaughter. Nancy's face was positively bloodless, and her eyes looked glazed over. The girl needed to be taken home and put to bed, not grilled by River Bend's sole lawman. "Sheriff, please, she's had a great fright, stumbling upon Grace like that. I'll keep her with me if you're worried she'll leave town."

"I'm sorry, ma'am, but I can't let her go yet," the sheriff responded. "I need to find out why she was there this morning."

"How is it *you* showed up at Grace's this morning?" Helen asked. She'd heard only that Mattie Oldbridge saw Biddle show up in his squad car with a well-dressed man just before Nancy ran out of Grace's house with blood on her hands. "Who was the man you said was with you?"

"I didn't say anything about him." Biddle leaned back in his chair and crossed his arms. "You must've heard that news elsewhere." He gave her a knowing look. "Besides, I'm supposed to be asking the questions—"

"Just as soon as you answer mine," Helen cut him off, patting Nancy's hand all the while. "The man?" she prodded.

Biddle sighed. "That was Harold Faulkner. He's Grace's publisher from the scholarly press in St. Louis. He claims she was supposed to meet him for dinner last night at Tony's in St. Louis. He was expecting her to deliver a copy of that book everybody's been gossiping about." The sheriff raised his bushy eyebrows. "You probably heard that news elsewhere already, too, huh?"

Helen scoffed. "Who hasn't?"

"Faulkner got worried when Grace didn't show," Biddle continued. "He tried calling her half the night and left messages on voice mail at her office and on her cell. He came into town first thing this morning and knocked on her door. When she didn't answer, he showed up on my doorstep. He was waiting here when I got to work. We went over to Grace's together," the sheriff said and shifted his gaze from Helen to her granddaughter.

"That's when you ran into Nancy," Helen said, squeezing the girl's hand as Nancy made a tiny whimper.

"More like she ran into me," Biddle corrected. "She had the bat in her hands. She dropped the thing at my feet, ma'am."

Helen bristled. "That hardly means Nancy killed her."

"Tell me, Mrs. Evans, what am I supposed to think?"

"That she was simply at the wrong place at the wrong time."

Biddle jerked his chin at Nancy. "I'd rather she explain it herself."

Helen started to open her mouth.

"In her own words," the sheriff butted in.

Helen turned to Nancy and crooked a finger beneath

her drooping chin. "Sweetheart," she said quietly, "can you talk about what happened this morning at Grace's?"

Nancy's pale eyes blinked. She looked numbly at Helen and then across the desk at Sheriff Biddle. She picked up the handkerchief in her lap that Helen had given her earlier, and she began twisting it into a knot.

"I didn't mean for it to happen," she whispered hoarsely.

"Nancy?" Helen's concern grew tenfold.

"Go on," the sheriff urged and leaned forward, seeming to watch the girl as closely as he listened.

Nancy ran her tongue across dry lips. "I didn't intend for Mrs. Beaner to get a hold of those notes. I tried to be so careful about everything. But Grace wouldn't even give me a chance to explain." She lifted her head, her eyes wide as she stared right at Biddle. "I waited for her at work, and when she didn't come, I thought something happened to her." Nancy faltered for a moment. "I still had a key to her house, so I went over and let myself in." Her voice rattled as she spoke, and her shoulders shook, as if she had palsy. "She wasn't downstairs, so I went up. Her room was dark, and I stumbled over the bat, so I picked it up.

"I didn't think twice." Nancy shook her head, glancing down at her hands. "Grace kept a baseball bat in her bedroom. I'd seen it there a dozen times before when I was over at her house, taking care of things. She was paranoid about living alone, just like she was paranoid about everything else." The girl lifted her chin, though her voice quivered. "I didn't notice the blood until I"—she stopped and sucked in a breath—"until I went into the bedroom, turned on the light, and saw her on the floor. I knew she was dead, and I flipped out."

"That's enough," Helen snapped, unable to sit a moment longer and watch her granddaughter be put through such torture. She got onto her feet and urged Nancy up. She wrapped a strong arm around the girl's shaking shoulders. "Nancy's not fit to do this, Sheriff. Even you must see that. I'm taking her home. She needs rest, not the third degree."

The sheriff raised a hand in protest. "Now wait a minute," he started to say, but Helen ignored him.

"Let's go, sweetheart," she told Nancy and guided the stricken young woman toward the door. "I'll be in touch," she said over her shoulder. Then, without another word, she led Nancy from his office and was gone.

Chapter 10

FRANK BIDDLE HIKED up his belted pants and started after them. He got as far as the door before he stopped himself with a shake of his head.

Helen Evans might be an occasional thorn in his side, sticking her nose where it didn't belong, but she was right about one thing: Nancy Sweet was in no condition to answer the questions he needed to ask her.

He went back to his desk and picked up the file on Grace Simpson. The facts in the case seemed simple enough. The psychotherapist had apparently been murdered in her own home, killed by a blow to the head. The time of death was likely before eight o'clock last evening, when she was supposed to have met her publisher in St. Louis. Doc's cursory exam at the scene showed rigor mortis had fully set in. The autopsy should help clear up any unanswered questions about the condition of the body.

But those results would take time, Frank knew. So, for now, what did he have?

Motives.

He tapped a pencil against the legal pad on his desk.

First and foremost was the book that Grace was to have delivered to Harold Faulkner. The whole town was up in arms about it. Anyone and everyone who'd been a client of Grace's seemed afraid they'd be turning up inside its pages, and that included Frank's own wife, Sarah. He'd seen how upset folks had been when they'd confronted Ms. Simpson at LaVyrle's last night. Frank couldn't help wondering if any had been furious enough about the impending publication to actually want Grace dead.

He chewed on the pencil.

What if one of those folks had gone to Grace's house and gotten into a hellacious argument with her? Then, in a moment of fury, had picked up the bat and slugged her hard enough to cause her death?

It was possible, he decided, and jotted down the thought. When he stopped scribbling, he let out a slow breath, his focus shifting back to Nancy Sweet. He knew little about the young woman except for the fact that she was Helen Evans's granddaughter. Nancy seemed a decent enough sort, but you could never tell how a person would react until push came to shove.

Take Lizzie Borden, he thought and pictured her friends' and neighbors' comments after the "forty whacks" she gave her mother and the "forty-one" her father. *She was such a nice girl,* he could imagine them saying and shaking their heads. *Who would have guessed she had it in her to do that?*

It happened all the time, Biddle mused with a sigh: a seemingly average person goes berserk and commits a most heinous crime.

Not that Frank was an expert on murder. This case involving Grace Simpson was only the second in River Bend, an occasional dead dog or deer notwithstanding.

But Frank knew enough about crime from his days on a city police force to realize that felons came in all shapes, sizes, and colors.

If Nancy Sweet had murdered Grace Simpson out of revenge for a job lost, she surely wouldn't be the first.

"THANKS FOR STICKING around, Mr. Faulkner."

"You're finished with the young woman, then?"

"For now." Frank sighed. "They take care of you over at the diner?"

"Good coffee, yes. I had half a pot, I think."

Frank flushed at the intimation he had kept the man waiting that long. "Take a seat, please, and we'll get on with the interview."

Grace's publisher took a gander at his phone before shoving it into his coat pocket. "I'm not sure where you want me to start," he said as he lowered himself into the chair Nancy Sweet had vacated not ten minutes before.

"Wherever you want to begin is fine with me."

Faulkner nodded, pausing as he laced his fingers in his lap. "Grace didn't arrive for our dinner last night, as you already know. While I waited for her, I had a couple of drinks at the bar and then at our table. I started to get angry, and I guess I got a little drunk as well. I'm a busy man, you understand, Sheriff. I don't have time to wait on writers who can't read the clock."

"I understand, Mr. Faulkner," Frank told him.

The man smiled. "Please, call me Harold."

Biddle studied the gray-haired fellow who fidgeted in the chair across his desk. He had lines about his mouth and eyes and creases in his brow that revealed a life well-lived. His suit looked nicely cut but was likely off the rack. The shoulders were a bit too wide, the cuffs an inch too long. Frank had looked up the scholarly press Faulkner ran, which was associated with a small-time university in the city. The titles they produced seemed too obscure to sell widely. No wonder the fellow was so anxious to get Grace Simpson's book. If it made readers outside River Bend as curious as the ones inside it, it might be the kind of hit that would push Faulkner's press well into the black.

"Every time I'd dealt with Grace by phone, Skype, or email, she was always prompt," Faulkner said, crossing his legs, then uncrossing them. "So it seemed out of character for her to be late, though I didn't have any cause to expect she'd met with such, er, grave misfortune," he went on.

Misfortune? Frank had to bite his cheek to keep from snorting. Was that how academics thought of murder?

"I waited a full hour before I gave up on her." Faulkner set his palms on his knees and fixed narrowed eyes on Biddle. "Grace Simpson might have been a lot of things,

Sheriff, ill-tempered, impatient, pig-headed, but she'd never missed any kind of appointment, at least not with me. Never."

"So Ms. Simpson was punctual but a pain in the butt," the sheriff said, which is how he translated the publisher's statement. "The two of you didn't get along?"

Faulkner's eyes widened, and his fingers began to fiddle with the buttons on his jacket. "I wouldn't say that, Sheriff."

"So you *did* get along?"

"Well, I wouldn't say that either." Faulkner turned his graying head this way and that, as if examining the walls of Biddle's office. He seemed particularly interested in a couple of notices about an upcoming farm auction in Jerseyville, Saturday's Grafton flea market at the old boatyard, and next week's River Bend town meeting.

Biddle cleared his throat and tried again. "You were saying that Ms. Simpson was tricky to deal with?"

"Ah, yes, Grace was quite her own woman," Faulkner replied, finally facing Biddle again, though now he played with the knot of his necktie. "She did things the way she wanted, and there was no room for argument. But she was innovative, too," he added, nodding to himself. "Her proposal for a nonfiction book about psychotherapy practiced in a county full of small towns caught my editor's attention and mine as well."

Biddle didn't interrupt. He jotted down notes as Faulkner spoke.

"We saw the potential for commercial appeal in Grace's premise. You can imagine that we don't hit the *New York Times* list often with academic tomes. We usually concentrate on titles by experts in various fields of education and science. Their work is often very dry." He tapped his fingers on the arms of the chair. "The subject matter doesn't make for a huge profit, of course, but we get by through sales to libraries and universities for the most part. Still," he paused, and his eyes visibly brightened, "I must admit I've always dreamed someday of publishing a bona fide best seller."

Faulkner let out a nervous laugh. "But then who in my field doesn't? I honestly believe Grace Simpson's manuscript has that potential. It contains elements of society's dark side, for want of a better description, which seem to engage the public. I'm saying this based on her proposal, as she refused to let my editor or me take a look during the writing process." His gray brows knitted. "Grace apparently wrote by hand and had her secretary transcribe. From what I understand, the manuscript wasn't even ready until sometime yesterday afternoon."

"So was this a deadline specified in her contract or just an arbitrary date?" Biddle asked, not sure of how things worked.

"Everything with Grace seemed a bit arbitrary," Faulkner replied with a snort. "As I said before, she was a tough woman to deal with, very temperamental." He tapped a polished oxford on the floor. "She believed this book would be her big break, and I think she sensed I felt the same for Faulkner Press."

"So did she cause trouble?" Biddle was finding this all very interesting. "Did she threaten not to deliver if she didn't get her way?"

"Oh, she threatened a variety of things," the man told him, nodding. "We argued quite a bit over her contract initially. She wanted a larger advance and cover approval, but all authors do." He waved a hand dismissively. "She didn't like the idea that we had the first right of refusal on her next nonfiction book."

Biddle rubbed his pencil against the side of his nose. "So, she got under your skin, huh?"

Faulkner grimaced. "Grace was hardly a favorite of mine, but I knew she wouldn't let me down."

"Until last night," Biddle said and ceased taking notes. "So you never got the manuscript?"

"No." Faulkner scooted forward in the chair, peering anxiously at the sheriff. "Would you happen to know where it is? If you wouldn't mind, Sheriff, I'd like to get a hold of it as soon as possible. There's such a hot market for nonfiction right now that the prime window for publication is sooner rather than later."

Not to mention the press that publishing a book by a murdered author might get, Biddle thought but kept to himself.

"No, I don't have the manuscript in my possession," the sheriff admitted. "But I imagine it'll turn up shortly."

"If the physical copy is missing, could you let me know if you uncover an electronic file?" Faulkner said. "Grace was afraid of being hacked, so it probably isn't on a hard drive. If it's been saved to a portable drive, I'll be happy to take that off your hands. With digital publishing, we could get the thing out next month if we worked fast."

"And I'll bet it'll go a lot faster without Grace around to get in your hair, won't it?" Biddle asked.

Faulkner flashed an anxious smile. "Harold, please."

"Won't it, Harold?"

Faulkner wiped his palms on his trousers. "Well, I don't think I'd put it as crudely as that, Sheriff, no." He glanced at his clunky wristwatch and grimaced. "Are you done with me, then? I need to get moving."

Frank set down his pencil. "You can go, Mr. Faulk— Harold," he said. "But I may need to get in touch with you again."

"No problem." Faulkner reached inside his jacket and withdrew a business card. "I'd like to help in any way I can. What a shock this all is. Grace being killed on the cusp of her big break." He sighed and pressed his fingers to his brow. "No doubt I'll have to issue some kind of press release about the matter."

"No doubt," Frank said, not hiding his sarcasm.

"Good-bye, Sheriff." Faulkner rose and extended a hand. Biddle rolled to his feet and reached across the desk. The man's palm was damp, the handshake blissfully brief.

Frank nodded. "Drive safe."

When Faulkner was gone, the sheriff leaned back in his old leather chair, wondering just how much publicity the little known Faulkner Press would gain by using Grace's murder to promote her forthcoming book.

Chapter 11

HELEN TIPTOED UP the stairs, wincing as each step released a protesting creak. She paused at the top of the banister and let her eyes adjust to the dim. She'd given Nancy a cup of Sleepytime tea and had tucked her into the double bed set under the eaves in the converted attic. When Joe had retired, he'd done most of the work up there himself, while Helen had polished the old wood floors, sewn curtains for the windows, and made the patchwork quilt for the bed.

When Joe had passed three years before, she'd been grateful for the extra room. In the weeks that had followed, Helen had found it helpful having others in the house. She'd been so used to hearing another voice, a pair of footsteps besides her own, or water running. But she'd gradually grown accustomed to being on her own, and she enjoyed the time to herself. She could do whatever she wanted to do, watch the TV shows she wanted to watch, eat whatever she wanted to eat. There was something to be said for not having to run on someone else's itinerary.

And she wasn't actually ever alone, not with Amber in the house. Though he might have four furry feet instead of two human ones, he held up his end of a conversation better than some townsfolk.

Helen heard a gentle moan come from the bed.

"Nancy?" she whispered.

But the lump beneath the bedclothes didn't stir.

It was nearly noon. Nancy had been asleep for hours already.

How exhausted she must be, Helen thought, though she could hardly blame her. After the trying events of the past twenty-four hours, the girl needed rest. Helen had insisted that Nancy stay at her house rather than go back to her apartment, and she planned to keep her there for as long as it took Biddle to solve Grace Simpson's murder.

Helen shook her head, sure the sheriff's barrage of questions had hardly helped matters any. As if stumbling upon a murder scene wasn't frightening enough.

I didn't mean for it to happen, she recalled Nancy telling Frank Biddle.

No, of course she didn't.

It's so unfair, Nancy had remarked after Grace had publicly humiliated her. *I've worked day and night to make her happy, and it was never enough. I hate her, Grandma, I do. I'm so mad, I could choke her.*

Helen frowned, knowing how hurt Nancy felt, how frustrated. But Nancy was a quiet girl who'd always worked hard and kept to herself. Even if she'd fought with Grace, she would never have picked up a baseball bat and beat her to death with it.

"Stop it," she told herself.

Nancy wouldn't hurt a fly, and Helen well knew it.

Unfortunately, Sheriff Biddle seemed to have his doubts.

The phone rang downstairs, twittering like a deranged bird, and Helen jumped.

She hurried back down the steps as quietly as she could, reaching the phone just as it twittered again.

Snatching it up, she asked breathlessly, "Yes? Who is it?"

"It's me, ma'am. Frank Biddle."

Helen gritted her teeth. "Sheriff, please, I told you I'd bring Nancy down when she was up and about. She's still in bed, sleeping."

"It's noon," he said.

"Thank you for that information," Helen replied, telling him, "good-bye." She was about to hang up when she heard him saying, "Ma'am, wait, ma'am!"

Helen returned the receiver to her ear. "Yes, Sheriff?"

"I just heard from Doc Melville, and it appears the murder was committed where the body was found, meaning Ms. Simpson's bedroom. There's no evidence the body was moved, so it looks like she died where she fell. Oh, and forensics confirms the murder weapon was the baseball bat that Miss Sweet was holding when she ran out of the house."

"So?" Helen said stiffly.

"So your granddaughter's fingerprints were on the

bat, ma'am. In fact, they're the only clear prints found on it other than Grace's. There are a couple of smudged prints that we're checking out—"

"Anything else?" Helen interrupted.

"Not yet, although Doc said the ME's about through with his examination. I'm heading over to Ms. Simpson's office now to see what I can find out there."

"Is that all?"

"Yes, ma'am, except that I'll want to talk to Miss Sweet again."

"Good-bye, Sheriff."

"Ma'am, wait—"

But this time, Helen hung up.

Chapter 12

"So it's true?" Clara Foley asked, leaning over the table.

"Oh, it's true all right." Bertha Beaner nodded.

"Ding dong, the witch is dead," Clara said and settled back into the booth, exhaling loudly. "Has anyone been arrested?"

"Mattie Oldbridge said the sheriff took Helen Evans's granddaughter in for questioning."

"Oh, my."

"Well, he had to." Bertha took a sip of her cola before adding, "She's the one who found the body."

"How was Grace killed?"

Bertha shrugged. "Mattie wasn't entirely sure, but one can't help but wonder—"

The door to the diner opened with a jingle, and Bertha Beaner stopped talking and glanced over Clara's substantial shoulders to see Mattie Oldbridge entering the place.

"Speak of the devil," Bertha murmured and lifted a hand. "Yoo hoo, Mattie!" she called and beckoned her over. "We were just talking about dear departed Grace. Seeing as how you live next door, well, we figured—"

"That you could fill us in on more of the details," Clara finished for her.

Bertha gave her a look and muttered, "I was getting to it, for God's sake."

Clara merely shrugged.

Mattie glanced wistfully at the counter where a brown bag awaited. "I just came in to pick up a sandwich and soup," she told them.

"Oh, come on, Mattie, spit it out." Clara wiggled her fingers, the nails painted the same vivid pink as her muumuu. "You must know something more than the rest of us. After all, you've got a front-row seat."

"Best seat in the house." Bertha chuckled.

Mattie shifted in her LifeStrides. "I'm not sure I know anything more than I told Bertha here this morning."

Clara pouted rosebud lips. "You didn't see anything else going on next door?"

"No." Mattie pushed at the bridge of her horn-rimmed glasses. "I haven't been outside as much as usual. This past week hasn't been an easy one, you know."

"Of course it hasn't, sweetie." Clara sidled down the bench so she could reach for Mattie's hand. "You must still be shaken after the break-in at your place."

Mattie tugged her hand away. "I am."

Bertha wrinkled her brow. "The sheriff hasn't caught the thief?"

"No," Mattie said, looking grim. "Whoever it is, he's still out there, waiting to strike again."

"I thought it was some kids from Green Valley," Clara remarked, "or that juvenile delinquent Charlie Bryan?"

Mattie sighed. "I'm giving up hope that Frank Biddle will ever find who did it. I'm sure I'll never see my precious things again. For all I know, they're behind the counter of some pawnshop in Alton," she added, eyes misting.

"And then to have Grace murdered just next door." Clara clicked her tongue against her teeth. "Do you truly think Helen's granddaughter had anything to do with it?"

Bertha cocked her head and listened.

Mattie looked from one to the other. "All I'm sure of is that Miss Sweet was the only one I saw go into Grace's house since I watched Grace leave in her car the night before."

"No one else went in or out?"

"I didn't notice anyone. I was having a beer on the porch after supper. But it was getting dark and my program was coming on the TV. That one with the dancing stars," Mattie said as Clara and Bertha both nodded. "There hasn't been much of interest going on at the Simpsons' place since Max moved out." Her wrinkled face softened. "He was such a sweet man, but she treated him so badly. Sometimes they shouted at each for hours so I had to wear earplugs to get any sleep."

"She and Max weren't legally divorced, were they?" Clara said and tapped a finger to her chin. "I wonder if he's going to collect all the earnings from her sordid book. . . ."

"Let's hope that book never sees the light of day!" Bertha's cheeks turned bright red. "If Grace hadn't threatened to divulge all those secrets, maybe she'd still be alive."

"Amen to that," Clara whispered.

But Mattie Oldbridge said nothing. She just looked longingly at the brown sack on the counter again.

Chapter 13

FRANK BIDDLE LET himself into Grace's office with a key from the ring in her purse. Her handbag had been found in her car, and it had contained her billfold, a tube of lipstick, a compact, her cell phone, and a handful of Kleenex.

Before he touched a thing, he pulled on a pair of latex gloves. Then he groped at the wall for a light switch. The overhead lamp flickered on, and he looked around him, finding himself standing in a small waiting room. The walls were sparsely hung with framed prints of what looked like blobs of ink, like something someone's kid might have done with black finger paint.

Chairs pressed tightly together lined the walls, with an occasional modern-looking glass table squeezed in between, its surface neatly covered with magazines.

Frank went through the door between the waiting room and inner office. He flipped on more overhead lights along the way. He first noticed a tiny kitchen set into a recessed spot in the wall. Or maybe "kitchen" was too fancy a word. It was more like a small cabinet on which sat a coffee machine, a tray full of creams and sugars, and a dozen floral mugs.

He opened the cabinet doors above to find office supplies, reams of paper, boxes of folders, and plastic-wrapped memo pads.

He walked ahead up the hallway, leaning into the opened door of a cramped-looking office. Was that where Grace had tucked Nancy Sweet? The space was hardly big enough for him to go inside and turn around without sucking in his gut. He decided to save that room for last.

Hitching up his belt, he continued past a framed poster of a staring Sigmund Freud to where a closed door blocked his path.

He opened it and stood inside the jamb, peering in.

So this was where Grace Simpson played headshrinker, he mused and let his gaze roam about. Sarah had told him it was nice, really fancy. *I think she must've had a real interior decorator from the city,* she'd remarked, her eyes wide as pennies. *So you've satisfied your curiosity, now you don't have to go back,* Frank remembered telling her afterward. But Sarah hadn't listened to him then any more than she ever did. Why his own wife couldn't have talked to him instead of coming here, Frank hadn't a clue. Maybe it was just one of those things women did that men never understood.

While her assistant's office was little more than a closet crammed with file cabinets and desk, Grace's domain was more the chamber of the queen.

The walls had been painted a rich cranberry, and the planked floor beamed with polish around the fringe of a plush, patterned rug. Behind slanted blinds, a wide window allowed an abundance of natural light in. The sunbeams glinted off gold frames mounted on the wall, the documents behind the glass stamped with seals and printed with graceful calligraphy.

Frank rubbed a hand over his head, ruffling the sparse hair that remained. Squinting, he took a look at each framed certificate, his lips moving as he read.

Bachelor of Liberal Arts in Psychology . . . Master of Social Work . . . Fully Accredited Member of the Psychotherapy Society of America.

There were half a dozen in all, enough to make Frank peg Grace Simpson as a bit of an overachiever.

There were shelves filled from end to end with texts, yearbooks, registers, and journals. He wondered if all the books were for looks or if Grace had read any of them. How much education did a person need to listen to people's problems and give them advice? Frank usually found the wisest minds weren't always the best educated but folks who had lived a hard life and learned from it.

A plush couch was positioned against one wall and above it hung a large unframed canvas that, to Frank's untrained eyes, looked like someone had accidentally splattered with paint.

Was that supposed to be art?

He harrumphed and hooked his thumbs into his belt on either side of his belly. He wondered how folks made money off pieces like that when he had a drop cloth in his garage speckled with just as much paint though he doubted anyone would be dumb enough to pay him cold hard cash to hang it on their wall.

A coffee table in front of the sofa contained a host of brochures that had been carefully fanned out. Biddle picked up a few and noted they dealt with all kinds of topics like codependency, aging, stress, and addictions of various sorts.

A pair of armchairs had been situated on the table's other side, the cushions comfortably worn.

But the sheriff didn't share his wife's interest in the décor. What interested him most was Grace Simpson's desk, which faced him from its cockeyed position in the corner. The piece looked heavy, with carved legs and ball-and-claw feet. A leather chair sat directly behind it. Biddle went around and plunked down onto soft leather. He tugged futilely at each desk drawer but only managed to work up a light sweat. They were locked, and, at the moment anyway, he had no keys for them.

He took out his pad from his breast pocket and pulled the pencil from its spine. He gave the tip a lick for good measure and flipped to a clean page, where he wrote, "Ask N. Sweet about keys to G. Simpson's desk." He found no appointment book among the papers on her green blotter and figured her schedule was probably computerized. He jotted a note to ask Miss Sweet about that as well.

Frank didn't see anything else lying about that warranted his attention, like client files or pages from the missing manuscript, so he tucked his pad and pencil back into his pocket, hiked up his belt, and headed for the closet up front that used to be Nancy Sweet's office.

He squeezed inside the limited space between the wall of filing cabinets and the desk. He could barely turn around and had to suck in his gut to attempt to pull open the file drawers; but like Grace's desk, they were locked up tight.

How, he wondered, could Nancy Sweet have worked here day after day and not felt claustrophobic?

When he tried the drawers to Nancy's desk, they thankfully opened. Frank riffled through each one, finding only the most ordinary of things: boxes of paper clips, staples, rubber bands, rolls of stamps, stationery, a jumble of pens and pencils. If there had been anything of importance in the desk, it wasn't there anymore.

Feeling defeated, Frank glanced above him then at a bulletin board tacked with countless Post-it notes. A number of them were addressed to Nancy, reminding her to pick up dry cleaning, to order St. Louis Symphony tickets, or to buy coffee and sweetener. The rest were for Grace, nearly all of them regarding phone messages from Harold Faulkner about her book.

He started to rise, but the space was so tiny that he got the leg of the chair caught on the wastebasket beside it, so that when he pushed back, he knocked the can over with a clatter. Trash spilled out all over his feet.

"Aw, damn."

He put the wastebasket upright and began to pick up what had fallen out: a gum wrapper, a few discarded envelopes, and a crusty bottle of correction fluid. He flattened out two messages that had been wadded into balls. One concerned a dental appointment for Grace the next week. The second mentioned an attorney calling about divorce proceedings.

Biddle stuffed the latter in his breast pocket.

Then he smoothed out a piece of memo-sized note paper.

> *Dear Grace,*
>   *You are a hateful, small-minded bitch, and it was hell to come in every day and work for you. I hope your book fails miserably.*
>   *Sincerely,*
>   *Nancy Sweet*

Interesting, Biddle thought, pushing back his hat and scratching his head. Was the note just a way for Miss Sweet to let off steam after Grace had canned her? If Nancy had truly intended to kill Grace, she would have been stupid to leave behind a message like that. Still, he folded the crumpled page and put it into his pocket.

He turned off the lights and locked up, rolling off the latex gloves and sticking them in his pocket. He was frowning as he headed back to his office.

Things weren't looking good for Helen's granddaughter, he mused. They weren't looking good at all. She had some explaining to do, more than he'd heard as yet, thanks in no small part to Helen's interference.

He'd get Nancy Sweet down to his office posthaste if it was the last thing he did, he decided, slapping his fist into his palm.

Only . . . only maybe he'd stop at the diner first and get something to eat. He figured interrogating a murder suspect was better done on a full stomach.

Chapter 14

HELEN SET THE cat food on the floor for Amber and watched him dive in up to his whiskers. Her twenty-pound tom had been pacing around her ankles and yipping at her ever since she'd removed a saucer from the cupboard. By the time she'd popped the top on the can, he'd gone bonkers. She wrinkled her nose as the smell of Salmon in Herring Aspic permeated the kitchen. It reminded her of the time she went to Florida one February at red tide.

She was rinsing her hands when she heard a gentle knock on her porch door, raps that fast turned more insistent.

"Mrs. Evans? Mrs. Evans, it's me, Frank Biddle."

Helen rolled her eyes heavenward or, in this case, attic-ward, wondering if the noise had awakened a still slumbering Nancy.

"Mrs. Evans?"

"Coming!" she called, muttering to herself as she wiped her hands on a dish towel.

She sidestepped Amber, who suddenly stopped gorging. He sniffed disdainfully and stared up at her as if to say, "You know, I'm just not in the mood for salmon in aspic. Would you pop the top on something else?"

"Not a chance," she told him in passing.

By the time Helen reached the porch, the sheriff had the screen door half open and was poking his head in.

"May I come in, ma'am?" he asked. Before she answered, he entered, allowing the screen door to shut with a gentle slap.

"Oh, please, do come in," she said wryly and, arms crossed, looked him over.

As always, Frank Biddle wore a slightly rumpled tan uniform, the belt of his pants hanging on for its life beneath a well-fed belly. He had his hat in one hand and smoothed down thinning hair with the other.

Helen didn't invite him to sit, but that didn't stop him from doing so. With a tense smile aimed her way, he ambled over to where a cluster of cushioned wicker congregated. He kicked out his dusty boots before him then cocked his head and said, "I figured that if the mountain wouldn't come to Mohammad, Mohammad had better head on over to the mountain."

Helen sighed. "I told you that I'd bring Nancy back down to your office as soon as she was fit. She's still sleeping, and I'm not about to wake her up."

Biddle shifted in his seat. "You don't seem to realize, Mrs. Evans, that this is a murder investigation, not a sewing bee."

Helen bristled. "I'm as aware of that as Nancy. But that doesn't give you the right to harass the poor girl when she's in a state of shock."

"Point taken," Biddle said, and he blushed. "But the first forty-eight hours are the most vital in a case like this, ma'am, and I don't want to waste 'em."

"Sheriff, I—"

"It's okay, Grandma," a soft voice interrupted. "I can talk now. Honest."

Helen turned.

Nancy stood inside the opened French doors leading out to the porch. Though her face was still pale and her eyes were underlined with gray, she did seem calmer somehow.

She came forward in rumpled socks, with a white terry robe covering her from knee to neck. Her hands disappeared in the deep pockets. She smiled weakly at her grandmother before taking a seat across from Biddle and drawing up her legs beneath her.

"All right, Sheriff," she said and sucked in a deep breath. "Fire away."

Helen stood beside the chair and set her hand on Nancy's shoulder, just to remind her granddaughter that she was there should she need her.

Biddle cleared his throat and gave his hat a final twist before he set it aside. "A witness heard you remark last night that you were mad enough to kill Grace."

"Bertha Beaner," Helen said and shook her head. "For

goodness' sake, Sheriff, Nancy was upset! And if I remember correctly, Bertha said she wanted to kill Grace, too—that Nancy would have to get in line."

"Ma'am," Biddle warned.

Helen shut her mouth, but it took some effort to keep it closed.

"Of course I didn't mean it, not really," Nancy replied, balling her hands into fists in her lap. "I was so frustrated with Grace. I'd worked my tail off typing up all her notes for her book, and then she fired me because of one mistake."

"Did you go to her house and argue with her?" Biddle asked.

"No, she was dead when I got there."

"I'm sure you didn't go there intending to harm her," Biddle pressed, "but sometimes emotions escalate and things get out of hand."

Helen was ready to shout in denial, but Nancy beat her to it.

"No!" The girl fiercely shook her head. "No, it wasn't me, I swear it. I didn't go over to Grace's house until this morning, right before I ran into you. Wasn't she killed last night?"

Instead of an answer, Biddle asked another question. "Speaking of last night, where were you between seven-thirty and eight-thirty?"

Nancy glanced up at Helen. "I was home."

"Alone?"

"Yes," Nancy insisted. "After I had dinner with Grandma at the diner, I went back to my apartment and shredded Grace's notes, pretty much all night, if you must know."

"So no one can corroborate your story?" the sheriff asked.

"No one except the shredder," Nancy whispered.

"Would you give me permission to search your apartment, Miss Sweet?" the sheriff asked. "If you have nothing to hide—"

"I don't," Nancy said and got up, disappearing inside for a bit and returning with her purse. She reached inside and plucked out a key chain. Her fingers shaking, she worked one key off and handed it to the man.

"Thank you, ma'am," Biddle said and tucked the key in his breast pocket.

Helen chewed on the inside of her cheek, fighting to stay quiet.

"Speaking of keys . . ." The sheriff leaned forward and set his forearms on his knees. "I was over at Ms. Simpson's office this morning, checking out the place, and I couldn't seem to find the keys to any of the file cabinets or to Grace's desk. Since those keys weren't on the ring found in her purse, I thought you might have them."

"Sorry, but I don't." Nancy sighed. "Grace didn't want those keys to leave the office, so she had me hide them."

"Where?"

"They're in the box of staples in my top desk drawer," she said.

Biddle pursed his lips. "Did she have an appointment book?"

"Yes, an old-fashioned one," Nancy told him. "She liked to make her own appointments, and she didn't like storing that kind of information on the computer. It should be in the left-hand drawer of her desk. That was where she kept things of importance."

"One more thing and then I'll leave you alone for now, Miss Sweet." Biddle reached inside his breast pocket and withdrew several slips of crumpled paper. He smoothed the first one out on his knee and passed it across to Nancy.

Helen squinted at it from over Nancy's shoulder. It appeared to be a pink memo of some sort.

"What do you know about divorce proceedings?" Biddle asked.

"You mean Grace's divorce from Max?" Nancy handed the note back and shrugged. "It was moving pretty slowly, I think."

"So this lawyer, Filo Harper, he's the guy handling things?" Biddle said and put the note back in his pocket.

"Yes." Nancy twirled a strand of hair.

"Was Max putting up a fight?"

Nancy stopped fiddling with her hair and sniffed. "I wasn't Grace's confidante, Sheriff. All I do know is that she was impatient to get things rolling after, like, a year of separation. She said she'd waited long enough to get him out of her life. That he'd gotten all from her he was going to get."

"Which means?" Biddle asked, and his brow furrowed.

Nancy threw up her hands. "I have no clue! Like I said, I worked with Grace. We weren't best friends."

"You're a bright girl, Miss Sweet," the sheriff went on, looking cross. "You must've picked up on more than what Grace told you directly."

Helen still had her hand on Nancy's shoulder, and she felt her granddaughter stiffen.

"I didn't spy on her, Sheriff, if that's what you're insinuating."

"Let's look at it another way," Biddle said. "Did her husband ever come by to see her at work?"

Nancy exhaled slowly. "I guess he did, maybe once or twice."

"Did they seem to get along?"

The chair creaked as Nancy wiggled against the wicker. "He cheated on her, Sheriff. Everyone in town knows that. It's why they were divorcing. So knowing how Grace likes to hold a grudge, I'd guess they probably didn't get along very well. Are you really through with me for now?" the young woman asked impatiently. "I'd like to take a long, hot shower and try to forget this morning altogether."

"Just one more thing," Biddle said and passed her the second piece of paper, which he'd smoothed out on his thigh. "Did you write this?"

"Oh," Nancy whispered, shoulders slumping, and Helen squinted to see. "How did you get that?"

The sheriff stared, unblinking. "I found it in the wastebasket by your desk."

This time, Nancy held the note for a long while, staring at it wordlessly before she turned her wide eyes up at Helen and then back at the sheriff. "I didn't write it for anyone to see. I was just letting off steam."

"Sure you were," Biddle murmured.

Over Nancy's shoulder, Helen read the message which began, "Grace, I despise you!" Oh, dear, she thought and swallowed, tightening her grasp on Nancy's shoulder.

"Surely, Sheriff, you don't think . . . ," Helen started to say, but Biddle raised a hand, stopping her.

"I'd like Miss Sweet to explain, if you don't mind, ma'am."

"I-I was angry," Nancy stammered. "I know it was a silly thing to do, but it doesn't mean anything."

"Under other circumstances, no, it wouldn't," Biddle agreed and reached out to take the paper back, though Nancy seemed reluctant to release it. He folded it and tucked it back into his pocket.

Helen had had enough. She let go of Nancy and came around the chair, her gaze narrowed on the sheriff. "Really, Frank Biddle, you can't actually think that silly note means she intended to kill Grace Simpson!"

"Your granddaughter was found at the scene."

"A mere coincidence," Helen said dismissively.

"Her fingerprints are on the murder weapon."

"Of course they were! She told you she picked up the bat."

The sheriff stood. "Grace Simpson's neighbor, Mattie Oldbridge, said Nancy was the only one she saw entering Grace's residence."

"Please!" Helen snorted. "Since she was robbed, Mattie's inside by dusk with her doors locked and all her shades drawn."

"She says your granddaughter looked fit to kill . . ."

Helen felt her cheeks heat up. "You know as well as I do that someone else could have been there before her. Grace could have been murdered hours earlier. For heaven's sake, Sheriff, she was probably dead since the previous evening. She must have been, or else she would have gone to her dinner meeting in St. Louis."

Biddle tugged his hat back on his head. "So maybe your granddaughter stopped by Grace's last night, argued with her, hit her with the bat, and left her on the floor in a panic. Maybe going by the next morning was an attempt to cover her—"

"Stop it!" Nancy sprang out of her seat. "Just stop it, the both of you!" She held her hands out in front of her, pleading. "I didn't do it, Sheriff, and that's the truth, whether you believe it or not. Everything happened just the way I told you it did. I don't have anything to gain by Grace's death, nothing." She dropped her arms to her sides then drew in a deep breath. She lifted her chin, but her quiet voice shook as she said, "Look, if you want to find out who killed Grace, why don't you go after someone who might have benefitted. Like those clients of hers who've been making threats on the phone, afraid their dirty linen's going to be aired in Grace's book. Why don't you start with the people who were gathered in front of LaVyrle's." Nancy met Biddle stare for stare. "Like your own wife, for instance."

"My wife," Biddle repeated.

"Yes, she was there," Nancy snapped. "So was Bertha Beaner, not to mention a couple dozen others. People who'd had enough sessions with Grace to fear their cases might end up in print."

"The book," Biddle said, changing the subject. "Do you happen to know where she kept that thing?"

"You don't have the manuscript, Sheriff?" At his silence, Nancy let out a *tsk-tsk*. "Grace had the only hard copy with her. She had me save it to a flash drive, which I gave back to her yesterday morning. If you find it, you should read it"—she paused and stuck her hands in the pockets of the bathrobe—"unless you're as afraid as everyone else that your deep, dark secrets are on those pages."

With that, Nancy padded away in her stocking feet, going back into the house. Helen heard her footsteps creaking on the stairs until all was quiet again.

Biddle started walking toward the door.

"Did you get the answers you wanted, Sheriff?" Helen asked. "Or did you end up with more questions?"

"Good day, Mrs. Evans," he said and nodded in a manner that was little more than cursory.

Helen watched through the screens as he got into his muddy black-and-white, the car spitting out gravel beneath the tires as he took off, leaving Helen to stare after him, a worried frown on her lips.

SHERIFF BIDDLE's visit left Nancy visibly shaken.

Helen found her upstairs, sitting on a corner of the

bed. She had her knees pulled to her chest, and she was gently rocking herself. She looked up as Helen stopped at the top of the stairs before crossing the room to sit beside her.

"He thinks I'm guilty," Nancy said, and Helen could see she was fighting to keep the tears from her eyes. "He thinks I did it."

Helen settled an arm around the girl and squeezed. "Well, he's wrong then, isn't he?" she replied. "Someone else must have been at Grace's house between the time she left LaVyrle's and eight o'clock, when she missed her dinner meeting. Despite what evidence Biddle seems to think he has, there's more to this than meets the eye." She forced a smile and patted Nancy's leg. "Don't fret, sweetheart. The truth will come out. It always does."

Even if I have to drag it out myself, Helen left unsaid.

"I wonder . . . ," Nancy murmured.

"What?"

"I wonder who really killed her." Nancy squinted in the dim. "Do you suppose it might be someone we know?"

Helen sighed. "It's an awful thought, isn't it? But highly likely, I'm afraid."

"What makes you say that?"

Helen shrugged. "There were plenty of people in River Bend who were upset about Grace's book, wouldn't you agree? I'd be hard-pressed to come up with a good reason why a total stranger would have wanted her dead. Unless—" Helen paused as another thought came to mind.

Nancy watched her. "What is it, Grandma?"

"Unless," Helen went on, "Grace's killer was a thief."

"A thief?"

"Someone broke into Mattie's just next door not a week ago, didn't they?" Helen said, finding that the theory didn't sound so crazy once she'd voiced it.

"Yes, but—"

"Bear with me." Helen sat on the bed and faced her granddaughter. "Did you happen to notice anything out of the ordinary when you went inside Grace's house? You'd been there enough before to be familiar with the place."

"I'll say," Nancy breathed.

"Well, was anything out of sorts?"

"I don't know." Nancy shut her eyes for a moment. "It's hard for me to picture much else except finding her like . . . like *that*."

"Try, honey, please."

Nancy tucked her chin atop her knees and stared off into the rafters. "What I remember is that no one answered the door, no matter how much I yelled and pounded. I used the key to get in, and the house was dark. There were no lights on, and it was quiet. When I went into the living room, I saw that Grace's writing desk was open. She always locked it, because it's where she kept important paperwork. Then I went up the stairs and into her bedroom." Nancy swallowed hard. "That's when I tripped over the bat. I picked it up without looking at it. Grace's clothes were a mess all over her bed, as though she'd dressed in a hurry and didn't have time to put them away. Maybe she was running late for dinner. Otherwise she would have straightened up. She was such a stickler about being tidy, you know, everything in its place and a place for everything."

"Go on," Helen verbally nudged when Nancy stopped.

Nancy's voice caught, and she blinked in the dark, reaching out for Helen. "I can't imagine that someone from town did that to Grace, left her there on the floor to die. . . ."

The words trailed off, and Helen felt her shudder.

"I'll never forget what she looked like."

"Hush," Helen cooed and raised her hand to smooth Nancy's hair. "It'll be all right, you'll see," she whispered. "Everything will be all right."

Helen couldn't bear to think otherwise.

Chapter 15

ONCE HELEN HAD made Nancy a grilled cheese sandwich and heated up some tomato soup—and encouraged her to actually eat the food—her granddaughter seemed far less agitated. Nancy was heading for the shower when Helen left the house, walking toward the river. She needed some time alone to clear her mind and think.

She followed the sidewalk past houses much like her own, clapboard structures with porches in shades of blue, yellow, and white; neat yards with pansy-trimmed pathways and, here and there, a picket fence.

Now and again someone would call out to her, and she'd smile and wave, though she never slowed her steps. She could only imagine what they'd already heard about Nancy, with Biddle pouncing on the girl like that. Helen's cheeks warmed as she imagined how fiercely the rumor mill was undoubtedly churning among the girls getting their hair done at LaVyrle's right this minute.

She drew in a deep breath. Never mind them, she told herself. Nancy was the one who concerned her, no one else.

Poor, poor Nancy.

Helen suddenly wished the girl hadn't come to River Bend to visit just after her college graduation. She wished, too, that Nancy hadn't found out about Grace Simpson putting up her shingle in town and searching for an assistant.

It's the perfect opportunity for me, Grandma, Nancy had said with such excitement in her face that Helen's chest ached at the memory.

A noisy starling cackled down at her from the branch of a towering elm. It sounded so chastising that Helen knew she had to stop blaming herself for the fix her granddaughter was in. She realized she'd curled her hands into fists, and she relaxed them. She slowed her quick pace as she reached the town's only chapel, sitting across a stone bridge.

She was close enough to the river to smell it, and her nose wrinkled at the fishy scent. Even still, she walked toward it, pausing only when the edge of town gave way to the Great River Road, a highway built along the Mississippi's edge. A century ago, the trail had been little more than flattened grass and railroad tracks. Now all that remained of the tracks were occasional forgotten patches of rusted metal overgrown with weeds.

Helen put her hands on her hips and stared at the brown of the river, at the boats skimming the water and the barges rolling through it, and she wondered how it must have been to stand on this same spot in another era, when steam-driven vessels had wheeled through the currents instead of noisy gas-powered speedboats that whipped this way and that, carrying women who wore very little and men belching beer.

She shook her head. Times had to change though, didn't they? And for the most part, she was happy about it. So much of what was new made life simpler. Other so-called advances only seemed to push civilization back to more uncivilized days.

If what was happening to River Bend lately—the unsolved burglaries and now the murder of Grace—was any indication, Helen wasn't so certain she didn't prefer the "good old days." If nothing else, life had seemed less intimidating.

A pair of cars raced up the highway, the sun glinting off the glass and chrome, and Helen shook her head at the noise and smell of fuel that lingered in their wake.

She clicked tongue against teeth, wondering what old Henry Ford would think of his invention now. It would probably make the man long for a horse and buggy. Why did it seem that everyone was in such a hurry?

Wasn't that why people like Grace Simpson thrived? Folks were anxious for a quick fix to their problems. They wanted someone to tell them what was wrong and to offer a fast cure, which often seemed to come in a little brown bottle.

It was too bad Grace had decided to use those confidences to her own advantage. Was a shot at fame so important that she'd risk betraying so many confidences?

Didn't she realize her clients would be furious at the idea? Didn't she understand that, despite the use of pseudonyms, they'd feel Grace was betraying their trust?

Helen couldn't help wondering if that was why Grace's husband had cheated on her. From what Helen had observed of Grace's stint in River Bend, the woman had seemed to care more about her career and personal gain than about nurturing relationships and healing fragile psyches.

A lot of good the book had done her in the end, Helen mused. All Grace Simpson's so-called ambition had gotten her was dead.

With a sigh, she turned away from the River Road and the Mississippi's wide brown waters, trekking along the sidewalk back into town.

Back to Nancy.

Chapter 16

SHERIFF BIDDLE DROVE slowly up the graveled road toward Amos Melville's place, the fifteen mile per hour speed limit allowing little more than a snail's pace.

As Doc's was only about two blocks away, Frank could have walked from his office instead of taking the car and probably made it there just as quickly. But Frank wasn't a man who liked to expend unnecessary energy. He'd been fit enough in his youth to huff and puff his way through his physical at the policy academy, but he'd never been one to jump on any of the exercise crazes that came into fashion. Jogging, he figured, was for the birds. Why, he wondered, would an intelligent human being want to run mile after mile if no one was chasing him? As for lifting weights, well, Frank felt strongly that if God had intended for him to pump iron, he would have attached dumbbells to his palms instead of fingers.

He braked the car at a stop sign where two tree-covered roads intersected, and he glanced to his right to see a figure in a blue sweat suit coming toward him.

Oh, great, he thought, exhaling slowly. He tipped his hat as Helen Evans leaned into the open window of his car on the passenger's side.

"Hi, Sheriff."

"Hello, ma'am," he said before turning his eyes back on the road ahead. He tapped his fingers anxiously against the steering wheel.

"Have you had a chance to look for Grace's missing manuscript?" she asked.

Biddle's throat tightened. "No, ma'am, I haven't, not yet," he said, but that didn't seem to make her go away.

"Have you questioned any of Grace's clients?"

"Look, Mrs. Evans," he told her as calmly as possible, "I'm on my way over to Doc Melville's to discuss the case. So if you wouldn't mind—"

"No, I don't mind a bit," she replied.

Without another word, she plucked her head out of the window and opened the door. Before Frank could make so much as a noise of protest, she slid in beside him, pulling the door shut with a loud *thwack*.

He let out a slow breath. "You can't go there with me, ma'am."

"I can't go to Doc Melville's?"

"No."

"Not even if I'm sick?" she said.

"You're not sick, ma'am," Frank responded, biting his check before adding, "unless there's a medical diagnosis for being a buttinski."

Helen turned to him, her blue eyes flashing. "If you don't let me ride with you, I'll walk there myself." The gray of her hair framed a face filled with enough lines to affirm her senior citizen status, but age certainly hadn't dulled her determination. "I have a right to hear what Doc and the county ME have discovered. It's my granddaughter you've accused of murdering Grace, after all."

Here we go again, Biddle thought.

"I haven't accused her of anything, ma'am, not officially."

"You could've fooled me," Helen murmured as she settled back into the seat and fastened the seat belt.

"Please get out, Mrs. Evans," Frank tried again.

She didn't even look at him. "No."

He heard the honk of a horn and glanced in his rearview mirror to see a dark Chevy pickup hovering behind the black-and-white. Biddle gave the man a wave before facing Helen again.

"Please, ma'am—"

"No."

The Chevy honked again, and Biddle saw the driver lean out his window to shout, "C'mon, Sheriff, the sign says 'stop,' not 'park.'"

"All right already," Biddle hollered out the window then turned to Helen.

"You'd better get a move on, Sheriff," she said, her eyes glinting in a way that told him she was amused without her having to smile.

He grumbled, taking his foot off the brake and pushing the gas. As he moved through the intersection, he realized he'd lost again. Helen Evans was going with him to Doc Melville's unless he bodily tossed her out. And Biddle figured he just might lose his badge over something like that.

So he did what he always did when Sarah drove him up the wall about this or that: he pressed his lips together in silence. Then he drove straight for Doc Melville's.

He parked at the curb in front of the A-frame where Amos lived with Fanny, his wife of fifty-odd years. Frank got out of the car and started around to Helen's side to open the door, but she'd already let herself out. She strode steadily up the path toward the side entrance to Doc's office. When he got to the door, she was waiting for him.

Above their heads hung an old-fashioned shingle lettered neatly with the words *Dr. Amos Melville, M.D.* The afternoon breeze pushed it ever so slightly back and forth.

Helen opened the door for him and waved him in. "After you, Sheriff," she said.

Frank didn't argue.

He doffed his hat and went on into the waiting room, nodding at Fanny, who was seated behind the receptionist's desk, alternately shuffling papers and typing on a laptop.

"Ah, Sheriff Biddle, right on time," the doc's wife remarked. She stopped typing and closed a folder, setting her hands atop it. "Helen? What are you doing here?" she added and peered above her bifocals. "Are you sick?"

"No, I'm fine," Helen told her.

Frank was tempted to ask if Doc had any kind of prescription that cured "bossy."

"I see." Fanny looked back at Frank again. "Amos only mentioned that you'd be coming, Sheriff. He didn't say a word about Helen joining you."

"It was kind of last minute," Biddle said, turning his hat in his hands.

"Yes, very last minute," Helen echoed.

"Well, if you'd just take a seat. Doc's in there with a patient. His last one of the day, thank the Lord. It's been a nutty week, for sure." Fanny shook her head, though the white cap of hair didn't shift an iota. "There's a strain of the flu going 'round, and then Jenny Patchett had her twins. And now with Grace Simpson . . ." She paused, sneaking a peek above her specs at Helen. "Anyhow, Amos's schedule's been booked up tighter than a tick."

"No problem, ma'am, we'll wait," Frank said and headed toward one of the dozen vacant chairs. He scooped a teddy bear from the seat and settled into it, putting his hat aside on the table. He picked up a battered copy of *Highlights for Children*, which he quickly set down again. Then he rummaged through new and old copies of *Parents Magazine, Modern Maturity*, and *People* until he found a *Field & Stream*.

Helen didn't join him. Instead, she went up to the reception window and leaned across it, talking in hushed tones to Fanny Melville, who turned her bespectacled gaze upon him now and then as they gabbed.

Sure that he was the object of their muted conversation, Frank ignored the whispers. As long as Nancy Sweet was under suspicion for Grace's murder, he had a feeling he'd probably get the cold shoulder from a number of Helen's friends in town.

It seemed an eternity before a slender young woman whom Biddle recognized as a part-time waitress at the diner emerged from the back hallway with Doc not far behind her.

"You'll be good as new in no time," Amos said to the girl, patting her bony shoulder as he slipped her file in front of Fanny. "Just go on to the drugstore, pick up the prescription, and start on it today. And Darcy, don't let Mary at LaVyrle's place glue on any more fake nails. Get a little water trapped inside those things and before you know it, you've got green thumbs for real."

"Yes, Doc," the girl said. "I got it."

Frank put aside the magazine and stood, hiking up his pants.

"Let us know if things don't clear up in a few weeks," Fanny was saying as the young woman took the written prescription from her and headed out the door.

"Why, hello, Sheriff," Doc said, removing the stethoscope from around his neck, rolling up the tubing, and stashing it into the pocket of his white coat. "I see you let Helen tag along. Did she hijack your car?"

"Something like that," Biddle grumbled, picking up his hat.

"Well, Amos, I could hardly stay out of this, knowing that my Nancy is the sheriff's prime suspect," Helen said, appearing suddenly at Frank's elbow. "You can't blame me for wanting to learn what else you've found out about Grace."

Amos rubbed his clean-shaven chin. "I can't imagine that what I have to say is going to help the situation much."

Biddle took a few steps toward the doctor. "Maybe we should go on into your office and discuss the matter privately," he said, though beside him, Helen bristled. "That is, unless you think it's all right for the ladies to hear."

Fanny Melville gave a snort and Helen sniffed. The meaning of each was equally clear.

Doc leaned a hip against the desk and smiled wearily. "I don't imagine it'll do them any harm to listen," he said.

"Okay, then shoot," Frank told him. "What have you got?"

Amos began slowly, as he always did. "As I told you already, Grace was killed by a blow to the head."

"From the baseball bat," Biddle interjected.

"Her occipital lobe was crushed. No doubt death was instantaneous."

Helen came closer. "And when," she asked, "was that exactly?"

"It's hard to pinpoint time of death medically," the doctor explained, "but as I told the sheriff here when I looked at Grace Simpson's body at the scene, the state of rigor mortis indicated she'd been dead at least twelve hours."

Biddle grunted. It was what Doc had initially suspected.

"See, Sheriff," Helen said triumphantly. "That means Nancy couldn't be guilty. When you found her with the bat this morning, Grace was already long dead."

"No, Mrs. Evans," Frank said, because this time the woman was barking up the wrong tree. "What it says to me is that Nancy argued with her after the scene at LaVyrle's. She had a key to her house. Mattie Oldbridge saw Grace drive off in her car around seven-thirty. Nancy could have snuck inside the house and waited for Grace to return. They fought, and Nancy hit her with the bat. Then she showed up again this morning, acting like a concerned employee to divert suspicion."

"That's insane," Helen countered.

Frank snapped back, "So is murder."

Helen did her best to stare him down, but he ignored her and turned to Doc. "Is there anything else?" she asked. "Sheriff Biddle said the bat had some partial prints on it. Are they running those through the system?"

Doc nodded. "Yep, and they're focusing in particular on seeing if Grace's husband's prints are on file." He looked at Biddle. "It's your theory they're his."

"So does Grace's husband have a criminal history?" Helen asked. "Why else would his prints be on file?"

Frank tugged his hat back on and rubbed his nose. "His sporting goods store sells firearms, ma'am, so he had to be printed to get a permit to legally sell."

"So that's it? There's nothing else that would help Nancy?" Helen looked at Doc hopefully.

Amos shook his head. "Sorry."

"Thanks, Doc," Frank said, giving him a nod. Then he faced Helen. "You need a lift home?" he asked out of courtesy.

"Thanks, but I'll walk," she replied.

The sheriff nearly sighed with relief; those blue eyes would have made mincemeat out of him all the way back to her cottage. He put his hand on the doorknob, about to leave, when Amos Melville's voice stopped him.

"Do you know what plans Grace's next of kin might have for her body?" Doc asked. "The ME wants to know what to do with it once he's finished."

Frank grimaced. "I don't know, Doc. I've been trying all day to track the husband down, but all I get is his voice mail. I called his store and was told he'd taken a few days off."

"Well, when you learn anything, give me a call," Doc told him. "The county morgue would like a heads-up so they can contact the proper mortuary when the time comes."

"Will do," Frank promised. Then he made a beeline for the door and escaped.

He went back to his office and sat down behind his desk, pulling out the file labeled "Grace Simpson." He spread it open on his desk and took out his pad of paper and pencil.

He didn't write a thing for a long while. He went over what he already knew—namely, that Grace was murdered sometime around eight o'clock the previous evening, give or take an hour. It wasn't a big leap to figure she missed the meeting with her publisher in St. Louis because she'd been murdered.

Had the therapist fought with Nancy Sweet? Could the young woman have smacked her with the bat—which she admittedly knew was in the house—and then left, perhaps not knowing Grace was dead. Had Nancy gone to Grace's house the next morning and made a scene just to cover her butt?

Nancy had no alibi for the hours in question. She had no witness to affirm she'd stayed home. Not even the pizza delivery man.

Frank set down the pencil and rubbed at his head.

Nancy's fingerprints were on the bat, along with Grace's. Did the smudged prints belong to Max? Maybe the bat had come from his sporting goods store.

Or had the partial prints been left by someone else?

And where was that damned manuscript that had everyone so riled up?

Frank put pencil to paper and wrote:

1. Track down Max Simpson
2. Go through Grace's office again—keys to file cabinets and desk in the staple box in Nancy Sweet's top drawer
3. Find manuscript!

He thought of Nancy Sweet's question about Grace's clients who'd threatened her before she'd died. Would one of the townsfolk have committed murder rather than risk a secret coming out? At least Frank knew where Sarah had been between seven and eight o'clock last evening: she'd been home with him, feeding him dinner.

It was imperative that he get his hands on Grace's

manuscript and that flash drive Miss Sweet said was the only existing electronic file. Frank figured he needed to peruse the unpublished book for himself, purely for the sake of the investigation.

With a grunt, he tapped the pencil against his chin, trying to decide where to start, how to make sense of this. If any sense could ever be made of a cold-blooded murder.

Chapter 17

HELEN WALKED HOME from Doc Melville's, trying to keep her chin up.

Could Frank Biddle honestly believe Nancy had clobbered Grace in the head with the bat last night and returned to the scene in the morning?

What the approximate time of death confirmed to Helen was that Nancy *didn't* do it. Helen was sure more than ever that someone else had been in Grace's house the night she died. But had it been someone she'd known or a stranger?

The sheriff had said there was no sign of a struggle, and Nancy had confirmed as much, remarking that the only thing out of place in Grace's home seemed to be the clothes strewn about the bed and the opened top on the living room secretary.

What troubled Helen most was the question of who had gone to Grace's unnoticed, and why.

The whole town seemed to know about Grace's appointment with her publisher. Did someone break into the house to lie in wait? But hadn't the sheriff said there was no sign of forced entry?

Helen stumbled on a crack in the sidewalk, caught herself, and glanced around, glad that no one seemed to be around to have seen.

She needed to watch where she was going, only she couldn't stop thinking about the case. One thing in particular kept sticking in her head: if Grace had left for St. Louis on schedule, as Mattie Oldbridge confirmed, why had she turned around and headed back?

What could she have forgotten that would make her return? It had to have been very important, Helen realized, and something Nancy had said fluttered into her consciousness.

She wouldn't let me email the book, can you believe? She wants to hand over the sole hard copy to Harold Faulkner in person.

What if Grace had forgotten the manuscript? That certainly would be worth her doubling back.

Tap, tap tap.

Helen started at the noise of fingers rapping on glass. She stopped where she was and turned to find herself standing on the sidewalk in front of LaVyrle's Cut 'n' Curl. Clara Foley stood behind the large window, smiling and beckoning Helen to come in.

Helen braced herself then pushed open the door and entered.

"Whatever are you doing wandering around with your head in the clouds?" Clara asked, expelling the words in a quick rush of air. She sat in the waiting area, wearing one of LaVyrle's purple capes. Dozens of tiny plastic rollers seemed to spring out of her head. "I was just chatting with Mary"—she wiggled her fingers at the girl behind the counter, who, Helen would bet, had done little actual chatting at all—"letting my permanent set, when I happened to look out and see you sleepwalking past."

As Clara spoke, Helen wondered how she could get so much out without taking a breath.

"Everyone's been talking up a storm about Grace Simpson and how the sheriff's pinned the whole thing on poor Nancy." Clara finally stopped yakking and pressed a finger to her double chins. "I don't buy it myself," she remarked, "though Mattie Oldbridge mentioned that Nancy looked pretty worked up when she showed up on Grace's doorstep this morning."

Helen knew the local grapevine worked fast, and normally she didn't mind. But the gossip usually wasn't about her granddaughter killing someone. "Nancy didn't murder Grace Simpson, no matter what Mattie Oldbridge thinks," she ground out.

Clara's hands fluttered. "Well, sweetie, of course she didn't."

"She simply had the misfortune to be the one who discovered the body," Helen went on, trying to explain, hoping Clara would circulate *that* information. "Sheriff Biddle doesn't have anyone else on his radar, that's why he's focusing on Nancy. He's had a lot of questions to ask her, as you can well imagine."

"Oh, I'm sure."

"Besides," Helen let slip what Doc had confirmed, "Grace wasn't murdered this morning. She'd been dead since last night."

Clara's penciled eyebrows rose. "Is that so?"

Helen nodded. "Nancy wasn't anywhere near Grace's house last evening around eight. She was at home."

"Alone?"

"Yes, alone!" Helen snapped.

"I see," Clara murmured, hardly looking like she believed that any more than Sheriff Biddle did. "So then Nancy's in the clear?"

"She is as far as I'm concerned," Helen said then muttered, "I just wish Frank Biddle felt the same."

Clara frowned and touched a hand to her curlers, the solution from the permanent dripping down her temples and onto the towel caught between her neck and the plastic cape.

"I should probably get home to Nancy," Helen said after a moment's uncomfortable silence.

"Wait!" Clara called after her as Helen started for the door. "Is bridge still on for next Tuesday?"

Bridge?

Helen stifled the urge to scream. "Good heavens, Clara, I don't know . . ."

"As if a little thing like death would stop the lot of you from playin' cards," LaVyrle said, high heels clicking on linoleum as she approached and stood with hands on hips, looking Helen over. "I must say, Mrs. E, you seem pretty frazzled."

"Oh, LaVyrle, you don't know the half of it," Helen started to say, but the beautician waved her off.

"Honey, I've heard the whole of it," the woman said, "about what happened to Mrs. S, I mean." Her usually unflappable tone sounded solemn. "It's awful, isn't it? Mrs. S was in such a fine mood when she was in yesterday. She was excited about that meeting she had in St. Louis with her publisher." LaVyrle shook her blond head and sighed. "It's a tragedy she didn't make it to dinner."

"Yes, it is," Helen agreed, ignoring the tiny snort that came from Clara Foley's direction. "She was a regular customer of yours, wasn't she?"

LaVyrle's red lips pursed. "She was, and I liked her, too. She had spunk in spades."

"Hey, LaVyrle," Clara said, wiggling her fingers.

"Give me a minute here, Mrs. F," LaVyrle said and turned back to Helen. "As I was sayin', what with the sheriff arresting your granddaughter and all, you're lookin' pretty stressed out. If you want, I'll have Mary give you a free conditioning."

"LaVyrle, please," Clara tried again.

"Another sec, Mrs. F, just hold your horses." LaVyrle grabbed hold of Helen's hands. She turned them up and down, bending over each as though studying each crack and crease. "Yep, it's just as I figured. Nerves show up in your hands and in your face. It's no wonder your nails are a mess. A good manicure would do the trick. I can have Mary fix you up real quick."

"Really, you don't have to," Helen protested.

But LaVyrle kept at her. "It's on me, Mrs. E. I'll have Mary give you the works: cuticles, massage, even a paraffin wax. So what d'ya say?"

Helen thought of Nancy back at home and shook her head. "As much as I'd like to, I should really be going."

"I insist." LaVyrle winked then called to the girl behind the counter, "C'mon, Mare, get your skinny rear in gear. Mrs. E's gonna have a manicure and paraffin wax on the house. You give her hands a good massage, too. She's all tied up in knots, aren't you, Mrs. E?" LaVyrle patted her with the gentleness of a bear. "Just relax and let Mary take care of you."

"LaVyrle," Clara whined.

"Yeah, Mrs. F?"

"I'm prickling," Clara cried and pointed at the curlers on her head, moving her neck around as though it had a crick; all the while, the permanent solution continued to drip down the sides of her face. "You said to tell you when it prickled."

"C'mon back, Mrs. F. I'll grab some gloves and get you rinsed out." LaVyrle guided Clara up the hallway toward the sinks, calling back over her shoulder, "Enjoy yourself, Mrs. E, you hear?"

Helen sighed as Mary came up beside her. "Does LaVyrle always get what she wants?" she asked.

"Always," Mary replied with a rare smile. "Are you ready for your manicure?"

"See what I mean?" Helen murmured and followed Mary's bobbing ponytail, taking a seat across from the helmet hair dryers. She settled onto the plastic-covered chair as Mary wheeled up a tray-table, plunking down on a stool on its other side.

For an hour, Helen allowed her hands to be massaged and rubbed with lotion, her cuticles to be clipped and cleaned. She even dipped her fingers into a bowl of heated paraffin, listening to Mary's assurances that the hot wax did wonders to soften skin and thinking only that her mother had used the stuff to seal the jars she canned her vegetables in.

Helen had to admit that if she didn't feel like a new woman when Mary was through with her, she at least felt like an old woman with new hands, which, she figured, was better than nothing.

Chapter 18

FRANK BIDDLE HAD barely been back in his office for two minutes when the phone rang. His encounter with Helen Evans leaving him grumpy, he picked up the receiver and barked, "What?"

"Sheriff? Sheriff Frank Biddle?"

"That's right," he said, hoping it wasn't a lost dog or a cat up a tree, anything that would take him away from his focus on the murder investigation.

"It's about my wife."

"Your wife," Frank repeated and picked up his pencil. He poised himself to write down the information. "Is she missing?"

"Not exactly."

"You have a fight?"

"Oh, we've had lots of them. Doozies," the fellow said and laughed.

Biddle put his pencil down. He frowned into the phone. "What's this all about? I don't have time for pranks."

"This is no prank," the caller assured him. "Like I said, it's about my wife. I've heard she died, you see, and I suppose I'm all that's left of her family. She doesn't have anyone else. She never did."

Biddle sat up straight. "What's her name?" he asked, though he had a feeling he knew the answer to that already.

"Grace," the man told him, "Grace Simpson. She was killed last night, from what I understand."

"And you're her husband?"

"I'm Max," the fellow said, "and, yes, by law, I'm still her husband. I guess Grace won't get that divorce she wanted after all, will she now, Sheriff?"

AN HOUR LATER, Frank Biddle stood face-to-face with Max Simpson.

Frank narrowed his eyes as he studied the man, and he straightened his spine self-consciously, although he realized it would take much more than that to make him equal Max's height. Max appeared to be in his forties, at least, though the only telling signs of his age were the brushstrokes of gray at his temples and the laugh lines about his eyes. He looked lean and fit in chinos, and Frank could practically see the lines of his six-pack abs underneath his sky-blue polo shirt. But then the guy managed a sporting goods store, Frank reminded himself. He should at least *look* like he used the equipment.

"You're a hard man to find, Mr. Simpson," Frank said and hooked his thumbs into his belt on either side of where his belly spilled over.

Max shrugged. "Sometimes a man's just got to take a vacation from life. I'm sure you know what I mean."

"Right," the sheriff said, all the while wondering what a guy like this had ever seen in a woman like Grace. Every time Frank had run into the therapist, she'd had her forehead bunched up and she'd been scowling. She hadn't had the best figure either, shaped more like a rectangle than an hourglass. Call him a chauvinist, but Frank had never given her a second glance. Could be Max went for the intellectual type. Grace had certainly had enough gray matter for them both.

"So, what's going on, Sheriff?" Max asked, and Frank ceased his scrutiny of the man, rounding his desk to take a seat behind it. "You told me over the phone that you wanted me to hightail it over here." Max spread his arms. "So now you've got me at your mercy. Is there something I can do for you? I don't want to get in the way of your investigation, if that's what you're thinking. No, sir, I'll keep my distance and let you do your work."

"Take a seat, please," the sheriff suggested, gesturing at the pair of them opposite his desk. "I've got a few questions for you."

It surprised Frank that Max didn't have questions for *him*. How many men whose wives had been murdered acted so nonchalant? Yes, Frank realized everyone reacted differently to death. There wasn't one set way to deal with grief. Only Max Simpson didn't seem to be grieving at all. In fact, he seemed tickled pink.

"Does this have to do with funeral arrangements?" Instead of sitting down, Max approached Biddle's desk and leaned forward. "Is there paperwork to be signed? Whatever you need me to do, I'll do it."

"Let's table the talk of funerals for now, all right?" Frank tapped his pencil against his chin. "She can't be buried until the autopsy's finished. So, please, take a seat," he said again.

"Of course," Max replied and finally parked his carcass in a chair. He stretched long legs out before him and settled his hands on his flat abdomen.

Frank noted that he glanced around just as Harold Faulkner had, eyeing the county auction announcements, town meeting reminders, and Most Wanted posters as though he'd never seen anything like them.

"I'm a city boy myself," Max said, though Biddle hadn't asked. "Grace grumbled about this place, but I think she really liked it. The whole 'big fish in a little pond' syndrome, I'm sure."

"Is that why she came here?" Biddle said, because it was something he'd wondered about ever since Grace had started her practice in River Bend. "I'd imagine there were many more folks in the city who needed her help."

"People need help everywhere these days," Max said and shrugged broad shoulders. "She was lost in St. Louis, actually. It took her moving out of the city to get what she wanted from her career. Only who would have ever imagined she'd end up roadkill in a tiny town like this? Who hated her enough to snuff her, Sheriff?"

So maybe Max did care about Grace after all.

Frank assured him, "That's what I'm going to find out."

Max sat up straighter. "I heard you've pinned the thing on that pretty gal who was Grace's assistant."

Biddle raised his eyebrows. "For someone who's just arrived in town, you seem to know an awful lot."

Max grinned. "Five minutes in the diner, listening to folks talk, and I know all the news that's fit to print."

Sometimes Frank wished the town grapevine wasn't quite so efficient. "Yes, Miss Sweet was brought in for questioning, but she's not under arrest."

"Is she the only suspect?"

"She's one of them." The sheriff frowned. "Let's just say that your wife wasn't real popular around here lately. I'm sure you know about her book."

Max shook his head. "What book?"

Frank waved his pencil in the air. "The one she was getting published by Faulkner Press in St. Louis. It details her time spent counseling in River Bend."

"Really?" Max looked incredulous. "She used to tell me that her clients were bumpkins and their troubles nearly put her to sleep. I'll bet a fortune she did a generous job of embellishing and made everyone's problems seem perverse instead of ordinary." He rubbed his square jaw. "I'm thinking sex with farm animals and such."

Frank tugged at his collar, discomfited by the turn of conversation. "If you don't mind, Mr. Simpson, I've got a few questions for you."

"Ah, Sheriff, my apologies," Max said, hardly looking contrite. "Ask away," he added with a sweep of his hand, and the toe of a suede oxford began to tap a relentless staccato on the floor.

Frank felt a headache coming on. "First things first. I need contact information where I can reliably reach you. I'm tired of talking to voice mail."

Max's mouth twitched. "Am I in trouble, Sheriff?"

"Only if you avoid taking my calls," Frank told him and pushed a piece of paper and pen in his direction.

"I'll be near," Max said as he scribbled. "I need to stick around for the reading of the will. You don't know when that'll be, do you?"

"No, I don't, but I'll bet it won't be any time soon," the sheriff told him, looking at the number and email Max had written down. "Like her burial, everything's on hold for a bit until we know something more."

Max leaned back in the chair and shrugged. "I'm in no hurry," he remarked. "It's pretty much a no-brainer that everything Grace had is mine."

The man sounded so sure. Frank cocked his head, saying dryly, "Unless you're the one who murdered her."

"Ah, a lawman *and* a comedian," Max quipped. Then he crossed his arms, looking suddenly serious. "Back to that book of hers you mentioned. I imagine I'll own the rights to it, too."

"You'll have to ask her publisher about that."

Max picked himself off of the chair and patted his muscled thighs. "So am I free to go? Or is there anything else?"

"Please, sit down, Mr. Simpson." Frank clenched his jaw. He was losing patience with the man. "We're not done yet."

"I'll stand if you don't mind," Max said. "This won't take much longer, I'm sure. I don't have anything to hide."

So Frank spit out the Mother of Questions: "Where were you between seven and nine o'clock last evening?"

He prepared himself for a blustery show of indignation, a sputtered, *How dare you, do you think I killed my wife?* but he was unprepared for laughter.

"Oh, God, where was I?" he remarked, guffawing and wiping tears from his eyes. "It's incredibly ironic, considering the reason Grace dumped me in the first place."

"Why don't you spell it out," Frank suggested, wishing he could slap handcuffs on Max Simpson and arrest him for being so cavalier about a murder.

"More fodder for the gossip mill," Max remarked airily and cast his gaze downward, flicking lint off his perfectly immaculate shirt. "I was with a woman who was not my wife," he said.

"Where?" Frank asked.

"Why, Sheriff"—a thin smile curled on Max's lips—"I was in her bed."

Frank's face heated up, but it didn't stop him from pushing the paper and pen across his desk again. "I want her name and number—"

"I'm sure you do," Max cut him off. But he wasn't smiling anymore.

"I'll need to check out your alibi," Frank said.

"All right, but she's a married lady, Sheriff, so be discreet." Reluctantly, Max came forward and picked up the pen, writing quickly and, Frank could tell from upsidedown, almost illegibly.

"By the way," the sheriff said before Max Simpson could bolt, "did you happen to leave a baseball bat at your wife's house?"

Max squinted. "Yeah, yeah, I guess I did. Grace said she kept it for protection, but I wonder if she didn't hold onto it just because it was a favorite of mine from my baseball days in college." He put his hands on his hips, nodding thoughtfully. "A solid maple Louisville Slugger, dense and not prone to flaking," he described as though reading ad copy from one of his sporting goods catalogues. "It's known for delivering a satisfying *crack* on impact."

"Is that so?" Frank murmured.

He suddenly got the strongest feeling that he knew the owner of the smudged prints on the bat that had fatally struck Grace Simpson. And he couldn't help but wonder if any of them were recent.

Chapter 19

DUSK SETTLED, DARKENING the room so that Frank had to get up from his chair and switch on the lights. He finished some paperwork and intended to head out. He wanted to get back to Grace Simpson's office before he called it a day and went home for dinner.

He was nearly to the door when the phone rang. "Sheriff Biddle," he said into the receiver, hearing his contact from the county crime lab on the other end. "What've you got for me?" Frank asked, and the answer was plenty.

Max Simpson's fingerprints were on the bat, all right, just as he'd suspected. There were several smudged ones buried beneath those of Grace and Nancy, along with a partial thumb. They matched up with a set on file with the St. Louis Police County Department, as Max's store was located in West County. Show Me Sporting Goods sold several dozen different models of firearms, from small-caliber pistols to hunting rifles. Max's prints had been logged with his permit to sell.

"Lucky for us," Biddle said, adding a "thanks" before hanging up.

He sat down at his desk, pulled out his pad, and scribbled down a few thoughts while they were fresh on his mind.

He'd forgotten to ask Max when exactly he'd last seen Grace. Or maybe it would be a better idea to ask Mattie Oldbridge. The old girl seemed to keep pretty good tabs on her neighbors, particularly since she'd been burgled the week before.

The sheriff mulled over his impression of Grace's not-quite ex-husband. Tall and good-looking, younger than Grace by a decade, and cocksure to a fault, he was hardly the picture of a grieving spouse. But then, Frank had heard they'd been estranged for quite a while, so there probably wasn't much for him to grieve about.

Frank pondered what Max had to gain by Grace's death.

For one thing, he spared himself the trouble of going through a divorce. Those could be costly and painful.

Would Max inherit Grace's house and her practice? Though Frank hadn't seen Grace's financial records, he had to wonder if she owned either free and clear. In this economy, he highly doubted it. Would a man like Max risk committing murder for Grace's money as well as her debt?

And what about the missing manuscript?

Frank wasn't sure he bought Max's ignorant act. How could he not have gotten wind of the infamous book when, in just one stop at the diner, he'd heard about Nancy Sweet being under suspicion for murder?

So many questions and so few answers, the sheriff thought and tugged on his hat. Then he ventured outside to the dusty black-and-white parked at the curb.

Gray-haired Agnes March was in the process of locking up her antiques shop adjacent to his office. She nodded and uttered a brisk, "Good evening, Sheriff."

He tipped his hat. "How do, Agnes."

"Have you nabbed the killer?" she asked and took a step toward him. She cocked her head and waited, studying him through her owlish glasses.

"Well, ma'am, I can't say that I have."

"Bully for that," she said and gave a little clap.

Bully? Frank wondered if she'd gone as cuckoo as those old clocks on the wall of her shop that he could hear going off every hour on the hour.

She smiled at his bemusement. "I think it's what they call the curiosity factor, Sheriff. Instead of scaring people away from town, they've been coming through like ants to a picnic. News of the murder's all over the Internet. I've sold twice as much today as I normally do this time of year. I heard a couple say they drove up from Springfield just to soak in the atmosphere."

"Huh," the sheriff murmured, hardly knowing how to respond.

Agnes marched up to him and patted his shoulder. "As you were then, Sheriff," she said, and off she went, heading up the road, the streetlamps seeming to glow brighter in her wake, though Frank knew it wasn't magic, just the falling dark.

He scratched at his jaw, hardly knowing what to make of the exchange. Had Agnes just insulted him? Or was it a compliment?

He recalled Max Simpson labeling folks in River Bend as bumpkins, and he knew that wasn't true at all. What they were, Frank decided, was quirky. Quirky with a capital Q.

He made sure he had the keys to Grace's office in his pocket before he got into his car. He drove the block and a half to the place and parked out front.

Once inside, he flooded the place with light. Then he pulled on a pair of latex gloves.

He went to Nancy's former office first and hunted in her desk for the box of staples. When he shook it open, he found the set of keys inside, exactly as she'd promised.

He entered Grace's cranberry-walled sanctum and sat behind her desk. Through trial and error, he found the key that unlocked the drawers. He didn't find the flash drive Nancy had mentioned, but he did locate Grace's old-fashioned appointment book.

He thumbed through the pages, stopping when he found yesterday's date.

Several familiar names had been penciled into morning slots, but they had angry lines drawn through them. Frank figured they'd cancelled, and he could hardly blame them.

"Beauty Shop" was penciled in at six-thirty and, at eight o'clock, "Dinner with Harold."

Frank flipped to pages for the days before, but nothing jumped out at him. Had he expected to find the killer's name written down in bold print?

He took his time going through the rest of her desk, turning up nothing of interest. Then he checked out the room again, pulling up couch cushions and feeling behind the rows of books on the shelves.

"Nothing," he said to himself.

He took the appointment book with him into Nancy Sweet's former office. He could go through the pages more thoroughly later.

Using the keys from the box of staples, he began unlocking file cabinet drawers.

The first drawer he inspected contained nothing but files about the office equipment and procedures, the bills for letterhead and envelopes, certificates for hours of credit at this seminar or that, a personnel folder with Nancy Sweet's job application, rolls of stamps, a zippered bank bag filled with petty cash, and copies of Grace's curriculum vitae.

The sheriff moved on to the two drawers below that one, finding they contained blue billing envelopes and insurance information, checks received and not yet deposited, checks returned from the bank, and letters sending clients with overdue balances to collection.

Frank marveled at the paper trail Grace's computer phobia had left behind, and he was suddenly grateful for it.

A folder stuck near the back with "SUIT" written on its label caught Biddle's eye, and he removed it from the pack. He flipped the file open and read a memo that had been paper-clipped to a stack of other pages, instructing Nancy to turn over copies of everything inside to her lawyer.

"Suit" as in malpractice lawsuit? Frank wondered. Did that happen to psychotherapists even though they weren't medical doctors? Frank squeezed into Nancy's desk chair and gave the folder a serious look-see. From what he could make out, the "suit" had to do with Grace billing a deceased client's estate. Scribbled notes mentioned the dead woman's children having been against Grace seeing their mother in the first place. So they'd filed a complaint against Ms. Simpson.

Unfortunately, Biddle didn't find that a motive for Grace's murder.

He put the folder back, then pulled the top drawer from the adjacent cabinet toward him.

Ah, here they were: her client files from A to Z. Well, from A to H, anyhow. He quickly found I through P in the middle drawer and Q through Z in the bottom one.

There had to be two hundred files, he figured, each one belonging to a separate client with a different name, different trouble, and, possibly, a motive.

Biddle sighed heavily, knowing he couldn't go through the things without a court order. If he needed anything evidentiary from Grace's client files, he'd have to get a subpoena. No prosecutor wanted a cop who had plucked fruit from the poisonous tree. Truth be told, Frank didn't really need to see the contents. He only wanted to confirm the names of a few of the townsfolk alleged to have seen Grace.

So if he happened to take a peek—off-the-record, of course—what could it hurt?

Instinctively, he looked around him even though he'd come into the office alone and was, as far as he knew, alone still.

Then he thumbed through the neatly typed labels on each file, seeing many familiar names, and learning more than he needed to know. Apparently Grace had seen not only the sheriff's wife but Bertha Beaner, wife of the chairman of the town board, as well. In fact, Frank saw so many names he recognized that it felt like he, Helen Evans, and the town's newly appointed minister were the only ones who *hadn't* sat on Grace's couch to spill their guts.

Feeling sick to his stomach, Frank gathered up the keys and the appointment book. He switched off the lights and got out of there, stripping off the latex gloves as soon as he got into his car. He drove the block and a half to Grace's house as fast as his beat-up car would carry him. If he couldn't find a copy of the book manuscript, then he was heading home.

He planned to have a few words with Sarah. If she had something to talk about from now on, he wanted her to talk to *him*.

Frank loved his wife, but he realized she was prone to gabbing too much and too often. And suddenly he found himself fearing that because of the blabbermouth he'd married, he himself might appear, however thinly disguised, in the pages of Grace's yet-to-be-published book.

Chapter 20

HELEN COULDN'T STAND it another minute. She had to do *something*. If the sheriff wasn't going to search for any suspects other than Nancy, then Helen was going to find some answers on her own.

Before she left the house, she fed Nancy dinner and settled her in front of the television. They didn't get cable here—it had to do with the way River Bend sat in a valley between the bluffs—but everyone had satellites. Helen had held out as long as she could, using rabbit ears on her old set and enduring grainy Cardinals games for years, until she'd finally caved, getting a dish on her roof and more channels than she knew what to do with.

But at least Nancy had found a show she liked well enough to stay put. The flicker of light cast ever-changing shadows on the girl's face. Even still, her features looked too pale, and her eyes stared at the screen, rarely blinking.

Helen shook her head. She couldn't blame Nancy for acting like a zombie. Until Grace's real killer was caught, how could anyone expect the girl to move on?

Of Helen's nine grandchildren, Nancy had always been the quietest and the quickest to blush. Helen thought of all the summers the girl had spent in River Bend with her and Joe. Ever softhearted, she'd brought orphaned cats to their doorstep—which is how they'd ended up with Amber—or butterflies with battered wings. Wounded frogs had found their way from creek bottoms into glass aquariums that had remained on the porch until the smell had gotten too much to bear. "A snake had it in its mouth, Grandma," Nancy would explain, tears in her eyes. "So I threw rocks until it let it go. It's missing a leg now, but if I just take care of it for a couple of days, it'll be hopping again in no time."

Helen smiled at the memory. Nancy was too kind, if anything. How Sheriff Biddle could believe the young woman could murder someone, even a cold woman like Grace Simpson, troubled her and frightened her at the same time.

Purposefully, she retrieved her windbreaker from the closet, pocketed a slim flashlight, and located the key to Grace's that Nancy still had in her possession—and which Biddle had apparently ignored. She had the screen door open when she heard Nancy's voice.

"Are you leaving?"

"Don't worry, sweetheart," Helen said, crossing fingers behind her back, "I'm just going out for a breath of fresh air. I'll be back before you know it."

Then she hurried out the door, down the porch steps, and into the night.

She walked briskly, pumping her arms as she went, hoping she could find something—anything—that Biddle had missed. Because as long as the sheriff held fast to his ill-conceived notion that Nancy had killed Grace, the real murderer went scot-free. That thought, Helen mused with a shiver, was hardly comforting in the least.

Lights warmed the windows of the houses she passed. Ahead, on Main Street, the streetlamps glowed cheerily above shops now darkened behind plate glass.

The diner had not yet closed, and Helen could see a dozen heads inside. She spotted Darcy, the young woman she'd seen at Doc's office, scurrying about in checkerboard pink. A coffeepot in one hand, she kept busy refilling cups.

Helen thought of something a woman she'd met at a bridge tournament in St. Louis had said to her upon learning she lived in River Bend. "My dear," she'd intoned, staring down her nose through glasses tinted pink and speckled with rhinestones, "what do you do to amuse yourself? I've heard tell the whole town shuts down after dusk."

Why, we country folk just settle into our rocking chairs, sip some white lightning, and listen to ourselves breathe till we're either too potted to care or fall asleep, Helen had felt like telling her if only to see the powdered-white skin flush. Instead, she'd ever so politely answered, "We do the same things as other people, I'd imagine. Watch the ball games on TV, play cards, or read a book."

"You read books?" the woman had said, her eyes wide.

"We even have a library," Helen had assured her.

"Is that so?" the woman had remarked, leaving Helen to wonder if in some folks' narrow minds, River Bend was akin to Siberia.

By the time Helen reached Grace Simpson's street, she was winded. She slowed her steps and slid her hand into the pocket of her windbreaker, feeling for her flashlight. As she passed Mattie Oldbridge's place, she looked up, recalling Mattie's statement to the sheriff that she'd seen no one come or go from Grace's after seven-thirty last evening, not until Nancy had shown up in the morning. Just as she figured, all the shades were drawn. Newly bought porch lights blazed, illuminating her rose bushes, as well as half the yard. No doubt she had one of her prime-time shows turned on loudly enough to drown out all else.

Helen felt reassured that Mattie hadn't been aware in the least of any visitors to Grace's the evening of the murder. The burglary had shaken Mattie so that she kept herself insulated once darkness fell. If she'd heard any unusual noise, she would have certainly called the sheriff and awakened him, even if it had been after midnight.

Helen went over what she knew to be true, the first fact being that Grace didn't make it to her eight o'clock meeting in St. Louis. Mattie had seen her depart, which meant that Grace had turned around and come back to her house unobserved. That surely implied that the murderer was already inside. Grace must have been killed shortly after entering, or else, as efficacious as she was, she would have called her publisher to tell him she'd be late. Clearly, she'd had no opportunity to do that.

Helen walked away from Mattie's brightly lit yard, crossing the width of a driveway until she stood before the shadowed lawn that belonged to Grace. She noticed that crime scene tape still crisscrossed the front door, so she flipped on the flashlight and slipped around the house, following the driveway toward the door in back.

And there was Grace's Ford tucked into her car port, too obscured by shrubbery for Mattie Oldbridge to see from next door. Helen shined her flashlight on the car. All the seats looked empty. The sheriff had mentioned finding Grace's purse inside.

She figured he'd checked the trunk as well, looking for the hard copy of Grace's manuscript. Helen found it quite odd that those pages had yet to turn up.

She approached the side entrance, settling her flashlight's beam on the knob. The brass looked dirty, covered with the graphite Sheriff Biddle used to dust for prints. Helen removed a key from her pocket, stabbed it into the lock, and turned it with a click. She was reaching for a tissue that she could use to turn the knob itself when a pair of headlights fastened on her. She jerked her head around as a car bumped into the driveway. Its brakes squealed as it pulled up right behind Grace's Ford.

Helen squinted against the brightness. She froze like a frightened deer caught on a back road. She had no time to hide, no chance to scurry off into the shadows.

The headlights cut off.

Helen's eyes struggled with blackness once more.

"Mrs. Evans? Oh, for cryin' out loud," she heard a familiar voice grumble. "What the devil are you doing here? Don't tell me you're breaking and entering."

"Of course I'm not!" Helen weakly protested. She held her flashlight behind her back, but she could hardly hide the key sticking out of the lock. "Well, I'm not breaking, anyway," she scrabbled to explain, "and I haven't entered yet, have I?"

"It's a good thing," Biddle growled, "or I'd have to arrest you."

He stepped around her and snatched the key from the lock, pocketing it. His hangdog's face glowered. "Ma'am, this is a crime scene. You're not supposed to come sticking your nose around here, especially at night. I'm conducting this investigation, you got that? I don't need your interference."

"Interference?" Helen sputtered. A jolt of fury rocked her. She was ready to let him have it again about just what she thought of his so-called investigation, but she stopped short and swallowed the angry words. "I just want to help," she said instead, her worry for Nancy overshadowing all else. "I thought maybe fresh eyes could find something that was overlooked."

The sheriff pursed his lips, staring at her for a long moment, and Helen was sure he was going to send her home or, even worse, drive her there himself.

But he sighed, his shoulders sagging. "I've already been through the house several times, and the county folks have taken all the photographs and fingerprints they're gonna take. So I guess it can't hurt if you come on in and turn on your spidey-sense." He crooked a finger at her. "Just don't touch anything."

"I won't," she promised eagerly.

The sheriff shrugged. "Besides, I'd like to find that manuscript of Ms. Simpson's. If you can turn it up, I might even deputize you."

Helen knew he was kidding, but she didn't care. At that moment, she could have kissed him.

"Okay," she said simply, afraid to say more for fear he'd change his mind.

He pulled a wad of something from his pocket and Helen realized they were gloves. With some fumbling, he snapped them on. Then he used a key from a ring to let them inside.

Helen followed him as he turned on the lights, asking something that kept nagging at her brain. "If the manuscript is still missing, don't you think whoever killed her took it with him?"

"It's a good bet, ma'am, yes."

"Then it couldn't have been Nancy," Helen remarked. "It wasn't in Grace's office, right? And you didn't find it in Nancy's apartment."

"No, I didn't."

"So you must have doubts," she pressed.

The sheriff looked at her and pursed his lips. But he didn't refute her statement, which Helen felt was an improvement. Maybe he was beginning to realize that solving Grace Simpson's murder wasn't going to be as simple as pinning it on Nancy.

"Let's split up, all right?" he suggested. "I'll head up-stairs. You look around down here. But remember—"

"Don't touch," she finished. "Got it."

He left her, and Helen decided she'd start in the kitchen. She did a simple walking inspection first, pacing the checkerboard floor and eyeing the pristine white counters. She moved into the breakfast room and rounded the drop-leaf table, a bowel of plastic fruit set-tled precisely in its center.

As she entered the living room, she inhaled a scent that wasn't unfamiliar. But she couldn't quite put a finger on it. Was it perfume? No, that wasn't quite it. She thought it might be a room deodorizer, though the vague odor made her somehow uncomfortable.

She spied the secretary that Nancy had said Grace always kept locked. Its desk had been pulled down, just as Nancy had insisted it was when she'd stumbled upon Grace's body. Had Grace left it open? Had something im-portant been removed?

Helen went over and peered into its depths. There were papers jammed into the cubbies. She figured the sheriff had already poked through them. There was noth-ing else that caught her eye.

She heard noises overhead and glanced up, knowing it was Biddle's footsteps, his weight causing the floorboards to groan.

Helen was walking through the dining room when Biddle clomped down the stairs and remarked with a sigh, "It's not here." He scratched his jaw, looking baffled. "It's like that manuscript vanished into thin air."

"The killer took it," Helen said, plain and simple.

Biddle didn't respond.

"Nancy wanted that book published," she told him. "She was practically the ghostwriter. No, someone else took it, someone who didn't want that manuscript to make it into print."

"I know where you stand, Mrs. Evans," the sheriff replied.

"If nothing else was stolen, then someone was in this house last night for one reason and one alone: to kill Grace and to ensure that her publisher never printed the book."

"Let's go, ma'am," the sheriff said and held open the door. "You want a ride home?"

"I'll walk," Helen told him for the second time that day, ticked off that he didn't seem to be listening.

"Fine," he replied.

And Helen stood alone on the stoop as Sheriff Biddle closed the door.

Chapter 21

MATTIE OLDBRIDGE PARKED her twenty-year-old Lincoln in the gravel and weeds by a chain-link fence. A dozen or so other cars already cluttered the makeshift parking lot by the river. Ever since some business-minded Grafton folk had decided to convert the old boatyard into a weekend flea market, the place never lacked for traffic.

Grabbing her pocketbook and sliding out from behind the wheel, Mattie smiled at the idea of people driving from the city out to this river town just to rummage through junk others had tossed out. And it was pricey junk at that. It seemed like anything that predated the Carter administration these days was called an "antique." Once Mattie had even seen a pair of mood rings from the '70s going for ten dollars each.

But once in a while, she'd find a real jewel: a lovely cherrywood table that needed only to be stripped and refinished, a crystal candy dish smothered beneath a layer

of dust, and a blue sugar bowl with a chicken filial. The
latter had been sold to her by a woman who'd found the
piece "distasteful," and which Mattie had since discovered dated back to the mid-nineteenth century.

She hooked her purse in the crook of her elbow and
walked across the rough ground. A slope of pavement led
downward to the opened doors of the barnlike structure
that housed the flea market.

Mattie stepped out of the sun and into the shadows of
the old boat works. A musty odor pervaded the cavern-
ous room, the smell of things trapped too long in someone's basement or attic.

Dozens of booths lined the walls and filled the middle.
Fellow shoppers meandered about, hunting for a bargain.
Music filled the air, dispersed by speakers near the front
doors, but Mattie couldn't even tell what song was playing. It was drowned out by the chatter of voices.

She took in as deep a breath as her lungs would allow,
then she plunged forward into the crowd. She had no
patience with paintings on velvet or glitter-glued sweat-
shirts or tables overstuffed with handmade crafts. What
good did it do to cover a roll of toilet paper with a cro-
cheted jacket? It wasn't as if the things could catch cold.

Mattie knew what she liked, and it certainly wasn't
that. Good glassware always made her look twice. A
gilded vanity mirror in great shape could inspire her to
haggle. She wasn't averse to buying a pretty rhinestone
pin or charm bracelet now and then, or even a sleek cigarette case made of sterling silver.

Mattie paused.

Could it be? Was it possible?

She picked it up and studied it, turning it upside down and checking the mark on the bottom. With trembling hands, she opened it up to find an inscription: "To M, Love H."

"Beautiful, isn't it?"

Mattie jumped at the brittle voice over her shoulder. She snapped the case back together and turned to the smiling woman who'd been watching her.

"How?" she began, but the word got stuck in her throat. She swallowed and tried again. "How did you get this?"

The woman lifted a hand to scratch at the red bandanna wrapped around her head. "It came from an estate sale," she told her, so smoothly that Mattie would never have guessed it was a lie if she hadn't known better. "It belonged to a well-to-do Alton woman who recently passed."

"Really?"

"Oh, yes."

Mattie held it to her breasts, which were heaving. She was furious. "No," she said firmly. "No, it didn't." She felt tears rush to her eyes. "It's mine," she told the dealer. "It was stolen from my house last weekend."

"That can't be," the woman said, but Mattie read the fear in her eyes.

"If you'd like, I'll call the sheriff in River Bend," Mattie said, lifting her chin. "He'll be here in no time flat, and he can confiscate the case and check the description against the police report I filed."

The woman glanced around her. A few customers inspecting items within her stall had overheard and stopped to stare. The dealer grabbed Mattie's arm, her mouth set in a grim line. "Look, lady," she ground out in an unfriendly whisper, "put the cigarette case back down and scram, all right? You're spooking me and everybody else. I'm sure you're just confused. You probably have that Old Timer's disease everyone your age gets."

Mattie took a step back so that her bottom bumped a table filled with mismatched pieces of china. The neatly stacked cups and saucers loudly rattled.

"I'm going to take out my phone and call Sheriff Biddle right now," Mattie said, her voice rising. "And when he shows up and proves this is stolen goods, that'll spook everyone even more."

The woman's eyes rounded, as if unsure whether or not Mattie actually had lost her mind. "I-I," she stuttered, wetting her lips, "I'm sure we can settle this quietly."

"No." Mattie patted the cigarette case, still folded fast against her bosom. "No, I don't intend to be quiet. For all I know, you're the one who broke into my house and stole it!"

"Me?" The woman put a hand to her heart, looking every bit like she was going to have a heart attack. By then, a crowd had gathered around them. "I didn't steal anything!"

"Then you shouldn't have a thing to worry about," Mattie told her, still refusing to let go of the case Harvey had given her almost fifty years ago, when the whole world had smoked and hadn't known any better.

With her free hand, Mattie rustled her phone from her purse and hit a button, speed-dialing the sheriff. Like clockwork, he showed up not five minutes after.

Frank Biddle's heavy boots clattered across the concrete floor as he entered the boat works and strode up the aisle toward the booth where Mattie remained in a Mexican standoff with the vendor.

The sheriff hiked up his pants and hooked his thumbs in his gun belt. "So where," he asked, "is the item in question?"

Mattie held the cigarette case out to him, a catch in her voice as she told him, "This is mine. It's one of the things stolen from my house. See," she said and opened it up to reveal the inscription. "Harvey gave it to me for our first anniversary."

Biddle took it from her hands and looked it over. "Sure appears to be the one you described in your report, ma'am." He turned toward the vendor. "I'd like to know how you got this."

"Well, I-I," the woman stuttered.

"She told me from an estate sale in Alton," Mattie said with a sniff. "And we both know that's a lie."

"I didn't do anything wrong." The woman's hands went to her kerchief-wrapped hair. "I had no idea this was hot, or I wouldn't have bought it."

"Just tell the truth, ma'am," Biddle asked.

"It was a boy, a teenager who brings me things sometimes," she explained, shaking her head. "Every once in a while, he has a few nice pieces he tells me belonged to his family. Says they're in a tough spot and need the cash." The vendor crossed her arms. "Lots of folk are hard hit these days, so it came across as real enough. The kid seemed decent, short hair, no tats, and he talked about living with his grandpa."

Mattie wrinkled her brow and looked at Biddle. The description sounded like someone from town, the boy who was always causing trouble.

"He had a crew cut?" the sheriff asked. "Was he about five foot six and wiry?"

"Yes, that's him," the woman said.

Biddle sighed. "Any chance he gave you a name?"

"Joe Smith."

The sheriff gave her a look like *You've got to be kidding*.

"I know, I'm a fool," the vendor admitted and gazed at Mattie with sympathy. "But if he's stealing, can you blame him?"

"Could you identify him if need be?" Sheriff Biddle said.

"Piece of cake."

"Well, if he should come by again, give me a call," he told the vendor and gave her his card.

"I will."

The sheriff nodded at Mattie. "C'mon, Mrs. Oldbridge. Let's head back to town. I'll meet you at my office."

Mattie followed the squad car along the highway to River Bend, although her oversized Lincoln moved more slowly than his cruiser. She went straight to his office and waited there, as he'd asked her to. Not long after, he showed up, dragging in Charlie Bryan.

Mattie had known the boy's grandfather for a good

many years, so Charlie was hardly a stranger. But he was familiar enough to the rest of the town as well, more for his antics than his parentage.

Biddle ordered the boy to sit in a chair across from his desk. Mattie stuck to the bench just inside the front door, not wanting to get in the middle.

"Did you steal this?" Biddle asked the boy point-blank, shaking the sterling cigarette case under Charlie's sunburned nose.

"What?" Charlie snickered. "Here we go again. I told you I didn't break into anybody's house, and it's the truth."

"That's very interesting," the sheriff said, perching on the corner of his desk so he towered over the seated boy. "A vendor at the Grafton flea market said she got it from a kid whose description fits you to a T. She's more than willing to come in and identify you."

"Okay." Charlie shifted in the chair so that one leg dangled over the arm. A beat-up tennis shoe jiggled violently. "So maybe I sold her the cigarette case. Big effing deal. That doesn't mean I stole it."

The sheriff shook his head. "C'mon, Charlie," he sighed. "How else could you have gotten it?"

"Maybe I found it!" He spat the words and jumped to his feet. He curled his hands into fists and raised his voice so loudly that Mattie put her hands over her ears. "I found it, all right? It was in the grass near the creek that runs behind the old lady's place. Somebody must have dumped it."

Biddle didn't appear to believe him any more than Mattie did. "Someone dumped it?"

Charlie stood his ground. "It's true."

There was something in his tone of voice that nearly made Mattie believe him. But then Mattie knew how easy it was for children these days to lie. It seemed to her that they thought nothing of it and no one taught them otherwise.

The sheriff stared at the boy forever and a day before he withdrew to a position behind his desk and settled into his chair. "You've been the one breaking into these women's houses, haven't you, Charlie?"

"No."

"Maybe you even broke into Grace Simpson's two nights ago, and she caught you," the sheriff suggested. "So you hit her with a baseball bat and ran."

Charlie stumbled backward. "No!"

Mattie tightly gripped her handbag, fingers trembling.

"I'm going to have to hold you for selling stolen goods, son," the sheriff said, his voice still unusually gentle. "You can call your grandfather and tell him where you are, and I'll talk to him, too, if he needs more explanation."

"You're putting me in jail?" Charlie kicked over the chair so that it cracked hard against the bare floor. "This is so effing messed up!"

Mattie covered her mouth with her hands.

The sheriff didn't even flinch. "You should thank your lucky stars I'm just putting you in a holding cell. It'll be a whole lot worse if I find out you killed Grace Simpson."

Chapter 22

LaVyrle's beauty shop buzzed with voices that fought to rise above the hum of the hair dryers. The persistent snap of scissors seemed to punctuate the chatter. The odor of solution for permanents and dye jobs pervaded the air, overpowering the sweet scent of shampoo and spray and the omnipresent tangle of perfumes.

Helen's senses throbbed at the discord the moment she walked through the door. The place was crowded even more than usual. "Come on in, Nancy," she called behind her and waved a hand to urge the girl inside.

"Helen!" someone shouted, and Helen saw Bertha Beaner sidle off a chair in the waiting area, leaving a pair of chattering women with their heads bent together. Soon enough, Sarah Biddle emerged from the back to join them, while Mary watched and twisted her ponytail behind the reception desk.

"Well, hello, Nancy," Sarah said, perhaps a tad too brightly. "It's good to see you."

The whispering duo in the waiting room instantly looked up as Nancy came to stand at Helen's side. Helen could feel the stares directed at them both, and she suddenly doubted her decision to bring Nancy to the salon for one of LaVyrle's special "perk-me-up" pamperings.

"Yes, it's wonderful seeing you out and about," Bertha remarked, as though Nancy had been ill.

Bertha looked much as Clara Foley had the day before, Helen mused. She wore the requisite lavender cape, and her head seemed wired with tiny pink curlers, around which a ring of white fluff had been tucked to catch dripping solution. The powerful smell of it caused Helen to wrinkle her nose.

"It's a lovely day, isn't it?" Bertha asked, trying so hard to force a smile that her cheeks resembled a chipmunk's. When Nancy didn't respond, Bertha glanced sideways at Sarah as if to say, *Hey, help me out here!*

The sheriff's wife quickly stepped in. "Don't let Frank push you around," she told Nancy bluntly, and her long face compressed. Even with lips pursed, her prominent teeth protruded. "You can't let him get to you. He's like a bulldog when he latches onto something. But he'll realize he's made a mistake with you and find the real killer soon enough."

Nancy cast her eyes to the floor.

Helen grabbed the girl's hand. "Of course he will," she said.

Sarah poked at the foil-wrapped strands in her hair. "It's just that he has to question everyone related to the case. It's his job to be thorough."

"So he's questioned the two of you then, has he?" Helen asked, not in the mood to mince words.

Sarah blinked and looked at Bertha. "Well, he did give me a talking to last night when he got home about my seeing Grace more than once without telling him. But he knows where I was the night Grace died, because I was with him. In my book, that's a rock-solid alibi."

"While we're on the subject," Helen said and nodded at Bertha, "Grace's book had you awfully worked up as well. I assume you've spoken with the sheriff?"

Bertha turned one shade darker than the lavender cape. "Are you suggesting that *I* murdered Grace Simpson?"

Helen blurted out, "Anything's possible."

"That's right," Sarah Biddle agreed, going on, "why, it could've been any number of people who hit Grace with that bat—her husband, Max, for example."

"Yes, or her publisher from the city," Bertha remarked, sounding miffed. "I heard that he hated Grace's guts."

"What about that awful boy, Charlie Bryan," Sarah added, looking around nervously. "This isn't for public consumption, but just this morning Frank put the boy in lockup after he found out Charlie had sold one of Mattie Oldbridge's stolen items to a dealer at the Grafton flea market. . . ."

"What?" Helen said, not having heard that tidbit yet.

Even Nancy raised her downcast head.

"Does the sheriff think Charlie's the one who's been burglarizing houses in River Bend?" Helen asked, wondering again if the break-ins and Grace's death were related.

Sarah's rabbitlike front teeth pulled on her lip. "Honestly, he isn't sure. The boy said he found the piece behind Mattie's house, like someone had dropped it."

Bertha let out a hardly subtle, "Hmph."

Helen glanced at Nancy. "You're right, Sarah, anyone could have done it. I just wish your husband was as open-minded as you."

Sarah sniffed, her eyes softening. "I never believed for a moment that Nancy was guilty."

"Nor did I," Bertha chimed in.

Nancy very nearly smiled for real.

"Thank you," Helen told them, seeing her granddaughter perk up a bit. "I just wish you could get your husband on the same page, Sarah."

The loud clack of approaching high heels effectively put an end to the conversation. LaVyrle appeared from her secluded station, bringing with her the smell of hairspray and Miss Clairol. She cocked her blond head and smiled tightly.

"Sorry to break up your gabfest," she said, and her dark eyebrows arched. "But it's back to the dryer for you, Mrs. B," she told the sheriff's wife, poking at the foil-wrapped strands in Sarah's hair with gloved fingers. "Five more minutes, you hear me?" she announced and tapped the face of her wristwatch.

Sarah nodded obediently before scurrying back to where her waiting hair dryer hummed.

"And you, Mrs. B," LaVyrle said, turning her attention to Bertha Beaner. "Let's check things out." She unsnapped a pink roller and unfurled a wavy strand. "Looks like you're just about done." She turned toward the lanky girl at the reception desk. "Hey, Mary, go rinse Mrs. B's hair, will ya?"

Eyes wide, Mary bobbed her head. With a squeaky "Follow me," she led the way to the sinks as Bertha Beaner hurried to keep up.

LaVyrle looked at Nancy and Helen. "So, Mrs. E," she began, "Mary said you called earlier. Your granddaughter needs a cut and blow-dry?"

Helen hugged Nancy to her side. "I thought she could use a little pampering."

LaVyrle winked at the young woman. "Well, I'm just the one to do it."

"How about a manicure, too, with the paraffin wax," Helen suggested. "That felt wonderful, I must say."

LaVyrle jerked her chin at Nancy. "How's that sound, honey?" she asked. "You want the works?"

"Sure." Nancy shrugged. "Whatever."

LaVyrle ignored her lack of enthusiasm. "We're pretty booked up today, but I can squeeze you in."

"Pretty booked up is an understatement," Helen commented, as the place seemed almost overcrowded. "Is there something going on tonight that I don't know about? Or has your reputation spread well beyond River Bend?"

"I'd love to say that's the reason." LaVyrle exhaled upward, blowing at blond bangs. "Though I think it's got more to do with morbid curiosity," she remarked and shook her head. "God rest her soul, but it's Grace Simpson who's bringin' them in. There's been more traffic today than I've seen in months. And what with that memorial service in the chapel tomorrow morning. . . ."

"What service?" Helen asked, yet another piece of gossip she'd missed.

Nancy's eyes grew wide. "Tomorrow morning?" she whispered.

"Heard it from Darcy at the diner," LaVyrle told them, leaning in. "She spent a while yesterday refilling Max Simpson's coffee cup, can ya even believe? He's hangin' around, waiting for the will to be read. So he figured he'd do a quickie memorial service at the chapel since he can't do a proper funeral yet, not without the body," the beautician explained with a wiggle of latex-gloved fingers. "He's not even puttin' a mention in the paper. Poor Mrs. S. She deserved better than what she got."

Helen glanced at Nancy, who gnawed on her bottom lip.

"Enough chitchat," LaVyrle said, seeming to pick up on Nancy's discomfort. "You ready, darlin'?" she asked and took Nancy's arm, drawing her away from Helen. "You put yourself in my hands, honey, and I'll doll you up real good. No long faces allowed at LaVyrle's. So how'd you like your hair cut? You thinkin' about trying a new style?"

Helen heard LaVyrle going on and on as she walked Nancy away.

Helen found an empty chair in the waiting area and settled in. Though she was surrounded by the cacophony of the salon, she hardly heard the buzz of hair dryers and drone of voices.

So Max Simpson had come to town, had he? And he'd decided to throw Grace a memorial service in River Bend despite the ongoing investigation?

He's hangin' around, waiting for the will to be read.

It sounded to Helen like the man had come out of greed, not love for a woman who was dead. All Max Simpson wanted from Grace now was to see what she had left him.

Chapter 23

HELEN WAS DIGGING into a third issue of the *Ladies' Home Journal* when the tippy-tap of LaVyrle's stilettos on the floor caused her to look up from the pages.

"How's it going?" she asked, hoping the "perk me up" pampering had actually done its job.

"Ah, we're just about done," LaVyrle told her. "Mary did up her nails real nice, and I gave her a cut. I added some highlights so she's got that sun-streaked look without havin' to spend all day outside pouring lemon juice on her noggin." LaVyrle went behind the counter and scribbled out the bill. "I even got her smilin' once or twice."

"Ah, you're a magician, LaVyrle. I tell you what." Helen set aside the magazine and stood. She walked over to the reception desk and leaned against it. "I don't know how the town would get along without you."

LaVyrle glanced at her sideways with blue-lidded eyes. "Well, until this mess with Grace dyin', it seemed like some folks did just fine. Half my old clients were doin' their own hair to save a few bucks, and it cut into my bottom line something fierce."

Helen sighed. "It's the economy. A lot of people have fallen on hard times."

LaVyrle sniffed. "Tell me about it."

"You're doing all right, aren't you?" Helen asked.

LaVyrle tossed her blond head and pressed her painted mouth into a smile. "And what if I wasn't, Mrs. E? Are you and your rich widow friends gonna throw me a fund-raiser?"

Helen slapped a hand against the reception desk. "You're darned right we would. All you'd have to do is ask. We could always raffle off one of Erma's handmade quilts." At LaVyrle's cocked eyebrow, Helen added, "Now don't scoff. We raised a pretty penny on the last one. It bought a new organ for the chapel, as a matter of fact."

"An organ, huh?" LaVyrle said and chuckled. "If you ladies got me one of them, I'd have your whole bridge club in here singin' 'Onward, Christian Soldiers' while I cut and colored the lot of you. I'd end up in the loony bin for sure."

"And we'd scare Mary to death," Helen said, joining in.

"It don't take much to do that."

Helen laughed.

LaVyrle gave the crowded waiting room a long look. "If things keep goin' like they are, I won't need one of Erma's quilts to get the Cut 'n' Curl back in the black."

"Silver linings," Helen told her, patting her hand. "What would we do without them?"

LaVyrle nodded.

Helen stepped around her and peered up the hallway. She could see a pair of heads tucked beneath the helmet dryers, but she couldn't see LaVyrle's private station from where she stood. "Could I check on Nancy?"

"Sure, go on back." LaVyrle looked up as a woman brushed past Helen to approach the desk. The lady raised her hands in the air, as if a victim in a holdup, though from the whiff of nail polish, Helen realized she was just fresh from one of Mary's manicures. "Tell Nancy I'll be there in a sec t' comb her out," LaVyrle said to Helen before she turned to take care of her customer.

Helen's sneakered feet squished softly on the vinyl floor as she made her way toward LaVyrle's boxed-in station. She reached the opened doorway and peeked around it. Nancy's back was to her. A lavender cape covered her from her neck to her bent knees. Fat hot rollers wound their way up and down her scalp.

Nancy's reflection stared blankly into the mirror. Helen summoned up a smile and swept in. "Hey!" she said and squeezed Nancy's shoulders, eliciting little more than a sigh from the girl's lips. "LaVyrle take good care of you?"

"I guess so."

"You like the cut, then?"

"It's fine, Grandma."

"And the highlights?"

"They're okay, too."

Helen brushed at wisps of hair curled upon Nancy's temples. "We'll go home in a minute," she promised. "LaVyrle just needs to comb you out. Can you hold on till then?"

Tears slipped from Nancy's eyes and rolled down her cheeks. "Yeah, I guess." The girl bit at her lip and nodded.

Oh, dear.

Helen dug into the pockets of her jacket but felt only the folded-up twenties she'd brought to cover Nancy's makeover. How could she have forgotten to fill up with tissues?

Nancy sniffled and wiped at her nose with the back of her hand.

Helen turned around to face LaVyrle's countertop. A box of Kleenex sat atop it, but the darned thing was empty. Helen tugged open a drawer below. "There's got to be a tissue here somewhere," she murmured, staring down at the mess of butterfly clips, hairbrushes, and combs.

She poked around with a finger. She found an unopened box of disposable gloves, the printed pad upon which LaVyrle wrote her clients' tickets, and half a dozen pale chunks of paraffin wax. One bore the perfect impression of a bobby pin, reminding Helen of a fossil. And then she struck gold.

"Ah-ha!" she said, locating a sleeved pack of purse-sized tissues stuffed near the back. She pulled it out, dislodging several plastic hair clips, which fell to the floor and clattered about her feet. A small photograph fluttered to the floor not far behind.

Helen dropped the pack of tissues into Nancy's lap, then bent to pick everything up, muttering all the while. She had the clips put away and the picture of a brown-haired boy in her grasp when she heard LaVyrle's angry voice.

"What's goin' on here, Mrs. E?"

LaVyrle stood at the mouth of the cubicle, hands on hips.

Nancy sniffled and wiped at her tears.

Helen tried to explain. "Nancy needed a tissue, and the big box is empty, so I just . . ."

"You decided t' go through my things," LaVyrle finished.

"I didn't think you'd mind," Helen said.

LaVyrle took a quick step toward her and snatched the photo from her hand. "I'll take that," she snapped.

"Who is he?" Helen asked as LaVyrle pushed the picture into the pocket of her purple skirt. But LaVyrle acted like she didn't hear and went about removing the rollers from Nancy's hair, her motions brisk enough to make Nancy wince once or twice.

"Is he your son?" Helen asked.

"I didn't say," LaVyrle replied, using her fingers to manipulate the brown waves so that they softly framed Nancy's pale face.

"I'm sorry," Helen told her. "I didn't mean to pry."

LaVyrle grabbed a tall can of hairspray from her counter and let it loose on Nancy's hair. Helen coughed as she breathed in the cloud.

"Look, Mrs. E," the beautician said when she finally

put the can down, "all everyone who comes in here does is yap, yap, yap, telling me who's sleepin' with who, who's split up, who's headin' to Florida when the first snow falls. No one pays t' listen to me gab about my life or my troubles. And that's just the way I like it."

Helen's cheeks warmed. "I understand, LaVyrle. Your life is certainly your own."

LaVyrle popped open the snaps on Nancy's lavender cape. "You can pay up front, Mrs. E. I already got your bill written out. Mary'll take care of it."

"LaVyrle, I—"

But the beautician didn't even glance up. She busied herself with a broom, sweeping hanks of fallen hair across the floor.

Helen took Nancy's arm and headed out, all the while silently chastising herself for being so nosy. If LaVyrle wanted to keep her private life to herself, it certainly wasn't her business to pry.

Chapter 24

No matter how many times Helen assured Nancy it wasn't necessary, her granddaughter insisted she was attending the memorial service for Grace Simpson the next morning.

Indeed, when Helen awoke just after dawn—with the weight of a very hungry Amber standing on her chest—she found Nancy already seated at the kitchen table, sipping a cup of coffee. The watch on Helen's wrist told her it was five minutes past seven, yet Nancy was dressed in black jeans and a crisp white blouse.

The girl glanced down at her outfit as Helen stared. "I know, it's not exactly a little black dress, but these are the nicest clothes I packed, and I don't want to have to go back to my apartment."

"No," Helen said.

Nancy wrinkled her brow. "You think I should change?"

"No, I mean, you can't go," Helen said and sat down at the table beside her. "Grace treated you terribly!"

"But I need to, Grandma, can't you see?"

No, Helen didn't see at all.

"The sheriff thinks you killed her. If you show up at the service, people will talk, and it'll only shake you up even more."

Nancy ran a finger around the rim of the coffee mug. "I'm not worried about what people say."

Helen shook her head. "You'd be better off going back to bed."

But Nancy stood firm. "This isn't for Grace, Grandma. It's something I have to do for myself. I need some closure, don't you understand?"

Helen didn't. When the sheriff found the real killer and put him in handcuffs, now *that* would be closure.

Why on earth would the girl want to go pay tribute to a woman who'd treated her like a minion, not a valued employee?

"Whatever's best for you, sweetheart," she told her granddaughter and smiled, though she wished she could find a rope and tie Nancy to the chair so she couldn't go anywhere all morning.

"Thanks, Grandma," Nancy said and got up. She went to the sink and rinsed out her mug before she headed up the creaking attic stairs.

Helen started to get up but tripped over the giant lump of fur that had silently come to sit by her feet.

"Amber," she scolded, her heart thumping, relieved she hadn't fallen and broken a hip. The oversized tomcat dogged her heels until she opened a can of Seafood Surprise and arranged the food on a saucer.

As she set it on the floor, she gave the cat's head a pat, thinking she had as much luck getting Amber to do what she wanted as Nancy.

"Why doesn't anyone ever listen to me?" she asked.

Amber sniffed the smelly blob of Seafood Surprise that was his breakfast. Then he tipped his head up and stared at her with marble-sized yellow eyes.

"No," she told him and wagged a finger. "I am *not* opening another can. You gobbled up this kind last week, so I bought a case of the stuff. How was I to know you'd change your mind so fast?"

Amber looked down at his saucer then up at Helen again. With an unhappy swish of his tail, he padded out of the room.

Helen threw up her hands

RIVER BEND'S NONDENOMINATIONAL chapel sat atop a mound of grass across a stone bridge that spanned a running creek. Whitewashed, with black trim, its pointed spire seemed to rise into the treetops that climbed the bluffs around it.

The gentle noise of an organ thumped the air as Helen approached. Nancy gripped her arm so tightly that Helen felt as though she'd lost all blood flow.

Helen determined from the persistent—though sometimes awkward—progress of the chords that the hymn was "Nearer My God to Thee," the tune played on the *Ti-*

tanic as it sank, one that Emma MacGregor seemed to play at every funeral service Helen had ever attended in the chapel.

The chords coughed from opened windows and hung upon the morning breeze in wheezing gasps, causing Helen to wince as she stood there, listening. But then Emma was nearly ninety if she was a day, and her arthritic fingers swelled enough to challenge her skills at organ playing. Still, Helen couldn't imagine not having Emma at the keyboard, trudging through each piece, feet pumping the pedals madly.

The wind tugged at Helen's hair as she crossed the bridge with Nancy and advanced toward the brief stone steps leading up to the chapel's double doors.

The newly hired minister, clad in white robes, greeted comers with a damp handshake. "Good morning, Mrs. Evans, Nancy. We've quite a crowd this morning," he said, sounding thrilled.

Helen murmured a good morning as well before she entered the church with Nancy beside her.

A red carpet ran up the aisle between the rows of carved pews and led directly to an oversized—and not very becoming—photo of Grace Simpson. It looked rather like a driver's license picture blown up. To the right of the easel that held Grace's frowning countenance was the pulpit; behind it hung a large wooden cross with a crucified Jesus.

Helen thought it was no wonder Jesus appeared so sad and disappointed. She felt like a hypocrite attending the memorial service for a woman who had caused Nancy such pain. Helen knew she'd be a better person if she could forgive Grace, particularly now that Grace was dead, but she wasn't quite ready to let go. Joe used to say she had Irish Alzheimer's: she forgot everything except a grudge.

"C'mon, Grandma, let's grab a seat," Nancy whispered.

Helen wondered where they'd sit. The pews seemed ready to overflow.

She picked out the heads of Bertha and Art Beaner, Sheriff Biddle and Sarah, Clara Foley, and even Mary from LaVyrle's Cut 'n' Curl. Helen didn't see any sign of LaVyrle as she searched for her bouffant blond head.

There were many more faces she didn't recognize. Perhaps, she mused, they were Grace's colleagues or from her publishing house in St. Louis? She recalled Nancy telling her once that Grace had few friends and no family outside of Max.

Helen wondered what it must feel like to live so alone and then to die alone, too, and she managed to summon up a smidgeon of sympathy.

She squinted at a man who suddenly appeared through the door that led into the pastor's office. He was handsome, with a full head of dark hair touched gray at the temples. His dark suit fit him nicely, emphasizing broad shoulders. He spoke with a few people in the foremost pew and then looked up, and Helen's cheeks warmed as his eyes met her stare, catching her in the act. He smiled, the grin in sharp contrast to his suit of mourning.

"Is that Max?" Helen whispered to Nancy, who kept looking around, trying to find them a seat. "*He* was Grace's husband?"

Nancy shushed her and took her hand, drawing her toward the far side of a pew nearly hidden by a stone pillar.

The turnout was amazing for such an impromptu service, Helen thought as she squeezed her fanny into a tiny spot beside Mary, with Nancy scooting in after. As Helen murmured a "hello" to LaVyrle's assistant, she wondered how many of those present had gotten word of the service via the Cut 'n' Curl. The place was River Bend's own town crier.

Mary smiled shyly in greeting. The lank brown hair that didn't fit into her ponytail fell into her eyes. The rest she tucked behind her ears.

"Where's LaVyrle?" Helen leaned over to whisper as Emma MacGregor kicked the organ into a gasping rendition of "What a Friend We Have in Jesus," the music so loud that Mary seemed not to hear. She merely smiled a vague smile.

The minister walked up the aisle and turned around. Then, with a sweep of arms, he urged everyone up. Helen stood along with the rest of the congregation.

She glanced sideways at Nancy, but the girl was staring ahead at the big photo of her dead boss. Helen felt her heart stutter, wondering when things would get back to normal again. When would Nancy stop being a zombie and start to smile?

If only Frank Biddle would catch the killer and set everything to rights. Nothing would change until he did.

"What a friend we have in Jesus, all our grief and sins to bear . . ."

Voices rose around her, and Helen shoved away her thoughts to join the chorus.

"What a privilege to carry, take it to the Lord in prayer."

As the hymn came to a close and the pews of people sat down, Helen tried hard to focus as the pastor led them through the memorial service, speaking of Grace and her strength, her desire to help free others from their troubled lives. Even as she listened, she found herself thinking of the night of the murder. What if the killer was in the chapel right now, pretending to mourn the very soul whose life had ended with one whack of a Louisville Slugger?

Her arms filled with goose bumps, and she rubbed them up and down. Still the idea left her cold.

She thought again of the fact that Biddle had found no signs of a break-in. Had Grace let her killer in? Or did the murderer have his own key? Nancy had one. What about Max? If Grace had bought the house before their separation, he'd probably come and gone at will.

Helen's heart thumped, feeling like she was on to something. What was it Nancy had told the sheriff about Grace's saying that Max had "gotten all from her he was going to get"? Yes, that was it. Had she been giving him money? Helen heard he owned a sporting goods store in the city. Maybe he was deeply in debt. What if he gambled and blew his money on craps and liquor and women, the usual things that seemed to pull most men down? Could Grace have been providing him with a means to support his lifestyle, only to pull the plug when she'd found out he'd cheated? Had Max been on the verge of losing it all if she had divorced him for real?

Helen kept on riding that train of thought. What if Grace hadn't made up a new will following the separation? Wouldn't Max, as her surviving spouse, get whatever had been hers, lock, stock, and barrel? What if he'd seen murder as his only choice?

"Grandma," Nancy whispered, touching her hand. "Are you all right?"

Helen blinked.

"Your hands are freezing."

"I'm fine," Helen said, though her heart pounded.

"You looked freaked out for a moment there," Nancy whispered as the pastor's voice rose and fell. Someone coughed. Another sneezed. "You're not thinking that maybe I actually—"

"Heavens, no," Helen cut her off, knowing right where she was going. She'd spoken loudly enough that Mary fixed her with a curious glance, as did several folks in the pew before them. Helen lowered her voice. "I've never doubted you for an instant, and I never will."

Nancy laced her fingers through Helen's and squeezed hard. "I love you," she whispered, and Helen smiled. For an instant, it felt like everything was all right again.

Then the minister ceased his oration and introduced Max Simpson, who took his place at the pulpit. "What can I say about Grace?" he said and gazed up at the ceiling, lips pursed. "I'm sure everyone here knew how stubborn she was and how she could be like a bulldog with a bone, snarling if you tried to take that bone away."

Nervous twitters erupted, and Max grinned.

As quickly, he turned solemn again. "She could also be incredibly softhearted. She really did like helping others. When I met her, she was working pro bono cases in the city, and she'd come home crying, telling me how unfair life could be and how she wished she could fix all the broken people at once."

"Yeah, so she could send out a big ol' bill," Helen heard a woman in front of her mutter.

Max went on, "I'm sure most of you were aware that Grace and I were one of the broken things she couldn't fix. I made a mistake that she considered unforgivable. I just wish"—he stopped, brushing at his eyes—"well, I wish we'd had more time to try to work things out. I believe we could have. Rest in peace, Gracie," he said with a sob. "Rest in peace."

This time the woman in front of Helen murmured, "Good Lord, give the man an Oscar."

The minister resumed his place at the pulpit and brought the service to an end with an eloquent reading from the Book of Common Prayer. "Earth to earth, ashes to ashes, dust to dust; in sure and certain hope of the Resurrection unto eternal life. . . ."

When he was through, his "Amen" was punctuated by a chorus of such. Then Emma MacGregor began pumping at the organ again, her fingers poking stiffly at the keys in a dusty rendition of "Rock of Ages."

The pastor led Max Simpson up the aisle to the church doors, ahead of those who rose from the pews and followed after.

Helen slipped out after Nancy with Mary in her wake. As short as she was—Helen liked to say she was five foot five if she stood up very straight—she couldn't see much above the heads moving in a single surge toward the open doors. But she could hear the voices.

"So sorry about Grace . . ."

"What a terrible thing . . ."

"Such a shock . . ."

Helen wondered how many of Grace's clients were offering Max their condolences, all the while feeling relieved that Grace was gone and probably hoping that her missing book would never surface.

She wasn't sure what she'd say herself. So when she reached Max Simpson, Helen nodded and dryly uttered, "Poor man, you must be heartbroken."

Max didn't seem to read her sarcasm. His handsome features beamed down at her, and he took her hand, holding it up as if he meant to kiss it.

"So sweet of you to come, dear lady," he said so that Helen wondered if he'd really heard her at all. He seemed to be going through the motions, like an actor in a play. Which was what he looked like, she thought as she studied him carefully before slowly moving away. She saw a dash of Cary Grant in his height and his hair, in the way he carried himself, but his eyes were a bit too close set. And there was too much humor sparkling in them for such a solemn occasion.

When Max saw Nancy, those close-set eyes widened. "Ah," he said, "Grace's lovely assistant." He picked up the young woman's hand as he had Helen's, only something in his eyes looked different. "Maybe I could take you for coffee so we can commiserate?"

"No, thanks." Nancy turned a shade of green and jerked away her hand.

Helen felt vaguely nauseous herself.

"Let's go, sweetheart," she said, catching her grand-daughter by the elbow and pulling her away.

As they crossed the bridge with a swarm of others, Helen lost Nancy's arm, but she didn't worry. She figured they'd catch up across the bridge. Most folks paused in the grassy area beyond to chat as they always did after an average Sunday service.

But when Helen turned around and searched for the brown head with the sun-streaked highlights, she couldn't find her. Where the devil had Nancy gone?

"Hello, Mrs. Evans," a quiet voice said, and Helen found herself standing eye to eye with LaVyrle's girl Friday.

"Mary," she said. "I was surprised to see you here. Did you know Grace well?"

The breeze pushed at Mary's hair despite her attempts to hold it back. "Mrs. Simpson was one of our regulars." She shrugged and blinked her big brown eyes. "I did her nails at least once a month, and LaVyrle did her hair more often than that." She shifted on her feet, which turned slightly in at the toes. "Since LaVyrle couldn't make it, she thought I'd better come. And you know how LaVyrle always gets what she wants." Mary shrugged. "So here I am."

Helen nodded. "Yes, here you are. Is LaVyrle working on a Sunday? I thought the shop was closed."

"Oh, she's not at the shop, Mrs. Evans," Mary told her. "She's got another job she works part-time."

"Another job?" Helen recalled LaVyrle telling her that the Cut 'n' Curl had been on shaky ground until these past few days, when new customers had flocked in. Had she taken on more work to pay the bills?

"Please, don't say I told you." Mary pursed her lips. "She doesn't like for people to know."

"I won't breathe a word," Helen said, but she wasn't looking at Mary anymore. She'd spotted Nancy on the other side of the bridge, talking to Max Simpson.

The man seemed to have Nancy's arm in a death grip, and her granddaughter looked none too happy about it.

"Nancy! Hey, Nancy!" Helen began calling out, loud enough that a number of heads turned in her direction. Helen continued to holler until Max loosened his hold and the girl was able to squirm away.

When Nancy reached her, Helen drew her close and whispered, "What the devil did he want with you?"

"Please, let's just go," her granddaughter pleaded, more upset than Helen had seen her all morning.

As they walked across the graveled path toward the sidewalk, someone came running up the road.

"Sheriff Biddle! Sheriff Biddle!" a boy yelled as he raced for the chapel.

"There's a fire!" the kid shouted, waving hands in the air. "It's at Alma Gordon's. Her garbage is up in smoke!"

Helen panicked hearing the news. Alma's house was right behind her carport.

Without another thought, she started off, striding as fast as she could toward the corner of Jersey and Springfield.

By the time she arrived, she was out of breath, and so was the fire.

"Slow down, Helen, there's no need to fret," Alma said when she saw her. "I put the kibosh on it myself."

Wearing a plaid duster and Crocs, Alma stood not six feet behind Helen's carport in a patch of weeds, holding a dripping garden house. Beside her, a dented metal barrel belched malodorous gray smoke. Alma's crab-apple face looked up as Sheriff Biddle arrived with a crowd from the chapel in tow.

"There's nothing to see," Alma announced, looking perplexed at the size of her audience. "It was probably just a cigarette got thrown into the garbage and set it to smoldering."

Biddle hitched up his pants and stepped forward, picking up a stick from the ground en route. He coughed as he poked at the charred refuse. Then he wrinkled his broad forehead and reached into the bin, retrieving something from it.

"What's going on?" Nancy asked Helen, coming to stand beside her.

"I haven't a clue." Helen shrugged.

"What have you got there, Sheriff?" Alma asked as she rolled the hose around her elbow. "It's only trash, nothing to get worked up over."

But Sheriff Biddle's expression appeared worked up

and then some. His gaze roamed the sea of faces and settled on Helen's before shifting to Nancy's. "I do believe," he said, holding up a piece of paper curled and black around the edges, "that I've finally found the missing manuscript."

Chapter 25

"IT DOESN'T LOOK good for her, Mrs. Evans," the sheriff said grimly. "The evidence seems to be stacking up against her."

Helen couldn't believe what she was hearing! "But why would Nancy take the manuscript from Grace's house? And why burn it? She was looking forward to the publication of the book. She told me it could mean a lot to her career."

"That was when she was still Grace Simpson's assistant," Biddle countered, staring at Helen from across his desk. "When Grace fired her, all bets were off." He leaned forward in his chair, causing the hinges to squeal. "She didn't have a thing to gain, only to lose, which probably made her even hotter about Grace giving her the boot. Taking the manuscript and burning it was the perfect act of revenge."

"On top of murdering her, you mean," Helen said with obvious sarcasm.

The sheriff shrugged. "Anger makes people irrational, and irrational folks do crazy things."

"Come now, Sheriff!" Helen threw up her hands. She was thankful she'd left Nancy at home. The girl would have had a complete nervous breakdown if she'd heard Biddle's latest insinuations. "Nancy's too smart to have done something so stupid as to burn the pages in the trash right behind my house!"

"Smart people can do very stupid things," he said.

Helen tried to control herself. She knotted her hands, pushing them against her thighs. I will not blow up, she told herself. I will not blow up.

Twice she inhaled deeply and let it out.

"Pray tell, Sheriff," she finally asked and managed to keep her voice level enough. "When was Nancy supposed to have set that fire in Alma's garbage bin? She was at the memorial service with me when it started. She couldn't have run to Alma's to take a match to the manuscript and run back without being noticed."

Biddle cocked his head. "Ever heard of an incendiary device, ma'am?"

Helen balked. "You're not serious?"

"Or else it was just a coincidence," the sheriff suggested. "Nancy ditched the manuscript in the neighbor's trash, only to have someone toss in a lit cigarette just like Alma said."

Helen rolled her eyes. "Good grief."

"Don't look at me like that, ma'am. I'm only telling it like I see it."

Fighting with him wasn't working, Helen decided. What if she tried a different tack? "Really, Sheriff," she said, "isn't it all a bit too obvious?"

"Lots of crimes are that, Mrs. Evans."

"But think about it a minute," Helen told him, and he seemed to be listening. "If Nancy had wanted to sabotage the book, why wouldn't she have just tossed away Grace's notes? She was the one typing them up. Grace despised computers, so it was up to Nancy to get the book in shape for the publisher. She could have destroyed everything then."

"Nancy didn't get canned until Grace had the manuscript in hand," Biddle said and picked up a pencil. He tapped it on his desk. "And I haven't found the flash drive yet, so maybe Nancy destroyed it, too."

"What about Max Simpson?" Helen asked, since logic wasn't working. "He could easily have come to town unseen and used his key to get into Grace's house. He's smarmy," she added, not trusting him a bit. "You saw him at the memorial service. Didn't he seem like he was putting on an act, and a pretty bad one at that? Does he even have an alibi?"

The pencil Biddle had been tapping slipped from his fingers and fell to the floor. It rolled noisily across the planks before it stopped. Biddle cleared his throat. "Uh, yeah, I asked Mr. Simpson where he was at the time Grace was killed," he said, fidgeting in his chair.

"And?" Helen prodded.

"Er, he was engaged in an affair," the sheriff told her.

"With a woman?"

"Yes?"

Helen leaned toward his desk. "Who was it? Did you speak with her? Can she vouch for him?"

"I spoke to her all right." Biddle scratched at his jaw. "She's, um, the wife of a rather prominent St. Louis politician. She asked that I keep her name under wraps for propriety's sake. Unless the evidence shifts toward Max, I'm going to do exactly that."

"Max's alibi is a married woman and she's worried about propriety?" Helen harrumphed.

"Like you said, smarmy." He ran a hand over his thinning crown. "Look, Mrs. Evans, I'm not arresting Nancy yet. The investigation's still ongoing."

"Does that include checking out Charlie Bryan's whereabouts the night Grace was killed?" Helen got up from her chair and walked partway around his desk so she could better eye the heavy door she knew led to a pair of holding cells. "I heard you locked up that teenage hooligan for selling stolen merchandise."

The sheriff narrowed his eyes. "Sarah," he said without asking.

"She said he sold a cigarette case stolen from Mattie's and that you're wondering if he's the one who burglarized the houses here in River Bend." Helen kept going when he didn't interrupt. "You must be wondering if he also broke into Grace's house and found himself trapped inside when she returned home unexpectedly."

Biddle cleared his throat. "Like I told you, ma'am, the investigation's ongoing."

"And Nancy's still a suspect?"

"Yes."

"Because Grace fired her?"

"That and the burned manuscript," he said.

That was it. Helen gave up.

She started toward the door, then did an abrupt about-face when another thought hit her. "Have you considered that Grace's murder had nothing to do with her work at all? That maybe the whole to-do over the manuscript was just a lot of smoke and mirrors?"

Rather than wait for him to reply, Helen stepped out of the sheriff's office, onto the sidewalk, and into the sun.

Chapter 26

THE RIVER ROAD Tavern sat wedged between a bait shop and a gas station on the main drag in Grafton. "Don't blink or you'll miss the place," Max used to tell Grace whenever they drove north on the River Road to Pere Marquette State Park.

But unlike that speck on the map that was River Bend, Grafton at least had a couple of places to stop for a cold beer or a shot of Jack straight-up without being eyeballed by a gang of white-haired old ladies who figured you for an ax murderer and not just a guy out for a buzz. And after the memorial service for Grace this morning—after shaking the wrinkled hands of countless seniors who'd offered condolences and patted his shoulder—Max needed a drink, and a stiff one at that.

He waited outside, leaning against the rough brick of the tavern until noon, when its doors finally opened.

The place was blissfully empty when he walked in: dark and quiet and smelling like sweat and the stench of the river. But Max would've settled for less at a time like this.

They served battered catfish along with the booze, and he found himself ordering a sandwich and a scotch on the rocks. A half hour after, the food lay untouched and the scotches kept coming.

When a fellow Max had met at the chapel—Grace's publisher, Harold Faulkner—wandered in with a sudden burst of sunlight, Max had already made good headway toward sloppy drunk.

"Si' down, si' down," he told the man and waved an arm toward the bartender. "Hey, I'd like a drink for my frien' here. It's on me. Anything he wan's."

Faulkner shook his head, but Max ordered a scotch for him anyway.

Clearly uncomfortable, the older man took the seat across the table and fiddled with the buttons on the jacket of his shiny suit. When the barkeep sent over the scotch, Faulkner pushed it away.

Max wondered why he was there. He squinted at the man's face. Nice head of hair, he thought, and was that a Rolex he kept checking? "So you were Grace's pub—" He stopped to belch. "Uh, publisher," he finished.

"And you were her estranged husband?"

"So ya heard abou' me?" Max grinned, sloshing around what was left of his most recent scotch. "Why'd ya track me down?"

The older man studied his manicure. "I wanted to speak with you about the book."

"Ah, the mysterious book!" Max nodded. "So you've still got plans t' publish it? Ya think it'll sell a few copies?"

"I do." Faulkner avoided his eyes.

"If the thing ever turns up, eh?" Max murmured. He set his scotch down and leaned over the table, hanging onto its sides. "You an' Gracie . . . you get along? Or did ya end up wishin' like hell you'd never met 'er?"

Faulkner fiddled with the knot of his paisley silk tie. "She was certainly single-minded."

"Single-minded?" Max repeated, slurring the words. "Ya mean she was a bona fide bitch." Max tossed down the rest of his drink. He raised a hand to snap at the bartender. "Hey! Hit me 'gain!"

The guy shook his head. "Sorry, buddy, you're cut off."

Max blew him a raspberry.

Faulkner looked uneasy. "Have you spoken with Grace's attorney?"

"About her will?" Max stared into his empty glass. "I've been trying, but I jus' keep getting his friggin' secretary."

"I'm sure they'll contact you shortly if there's cause."

"If she lef' a will at all."

"Not leave a will?" Faulkner looked apoplectic. "Grace was so obsessive about details that I can't imagine she wouldn't leave instructions about everything."

"Oh, she was obsessive all right," Max agreed, eyeing the scotch Faulkner hadn't touched. "But she didn't like dealin' with law sharks any more than she liked computers. That's why the divorce was takin' so damn long. She tol' me once when she got rid of me for good, she wouldn't need a will to make sure I got nothing."

Faulkner ran a finger between his neck and collar. "But if you're not divorced and you're not arrested for her murder, then it would mean—"

"That I get it all," Max finished and grinned in a lopsided fashion.

"What about the book?"

Max laughed, reaching across the scarred tabletop to pat the man's hand. "Well, if that idiot sheriff ever finds it, looks like you'll be dealin' with me."

"But I assumed—"

"That with her out of the picture you'd have free rein," Max said. Through bleary eyes, he saw the man's Adam's apple jump. "Well, you were wrong."

Faulkner hardly appeared thrilled. "I hadn't counted on this."

"You mean, you hadn't counted on *me*," Max said and laughed loudly.

"I'll be in touch," Faulkner told him and rose from his seat.

"Like hell," Max called out. "*I'll* be in touch!"

The older man nearly knocked the chair over in his haste to retreat. He scurried toward the door, practically tripping over his shiny loafers.

A burst of sunlight invaded the dim as the door opened. Max cringed at the brightness, raising a hand to shield his eyes. He cursed under his breath until the gray of the room settled in again.

Then he reached for Faulkner's untouched scotch. He thought of Grace, and he lifted the glass. "To my dearly departed wife," he said before he knocked the liquor back so fast it burned his throat and tears filled his eyes.

Chapter 27

HELEN MARCHED OUT of Sheriff Biddle's office feeling as baffled as ever by the day's events. It was past noon already, she noticed, checking her wristwatch. She picked up her pace, her shoes tapping on the sidewalk as she headed past the McCaffreys'—and their barking dog—then by the Kramers' picket fence until she finally reached home.

Amber reclined on the green-painted steps leading up to the porch. He rolled onto his feet as she approached. His back arched as he stretched and his tail lifted straight into the air. He raised a paw to tug at the screen door, banging it against the frame as if to say, *For God's sake, woman, where have you been? Let me in!*

"I hope you had a better morning than I did," she told him and pushed the door wide. He turned his yellow eyes upward and blinked before he trotted past, his tail swishing as he loped toward the kitchen.

"Nancy?" Helen called as she came in from the porch. "Sweetheart, are you here?"

"Upstairs, Grandma," she shouted in reply.

Helen ignored Amber's howls—they were the "feed me now" kind, as opposed to the "pet me this instant" or "don't you think it's time for fresh kitty litter?" Grabbing hold of the banister, she trudged up the creaking stairs to the attic. She felt tired, she realized, but then she hadn't been sleeping well, and with good cause. Add to that all the running around town she'd been doing, and it was no wonder her knees ached and her feet felt sore. It was at times like this that she remembered she was seventy-five. She was supposed to be relaxing in her sunset years, not dogging the local sheriff in a murder investigation.

But then Helen figured she'd never been good at relaxing. Not even when she and Joe had vacationed. She was a doer. She wasn't good at sitting still. When she kept busy, she didn't feel like seventy-five; she didn't feel any particular age at all. She just felt alive. Doing the things she loved had kept her going after Joe had died. Why would she want to slow down now?

As she reached the top step, Helen paused, catching her breath and thinking of just how far she'd come after losing her husband. She decided she could get through near about anything after that, even Sheriff Biddle all but accusing her granddaughter of murder.

"Nancy?"

"In here," called a voice from within the bathroom.

Helen crossed the wood floor and poked her head in, expecting to find the girl soaking in a sea of bubbles. In-

stead, she found Nancy gathering her toiletries and stuffing them into a small canvas bag.

"What's going on?" she asked, pausing in the doorway. "You're not going back to your apartment already?"

"I think it's time I did."

"But it's only been a few days."

Nancy dropped a tube of toothpaste into the bag and
looked up. Her hair was drawn off her face by blue bar-
rettes, and her face was devoid of makeup. If she'd had
braces on her teeth, she would have looked exactly like
her thirteen-year-old self, not the twenty-three-year-old
woman she'd become. "I want to thank you for letting me
stay with you, but I need to get back on my own two feet."

"You've been through so much," Helen said, biting her
tongue before she added, *and it's not over yet.*

"Grandma, listen." Nancy ceased putting things in
her bag. "I'm okay. I really am. Being fired by Grace one
day and finding her dead the next threw me for a loop.
But I'll get through it."

"The sheriff thinks—" Helen started to say, unable
to forget her very recent conversation with Biddle in his
office. Despite professing to look at other suspects, he still
had his sights set on Nancy.

"I'm not worried about him," Nancy said. "He'll find
who really killed Grace sooner or later, and he'll realize I
had nothing to do with it."

"Of course he will."

"Of course," Nancy echoed. She picked up her canvas
bag and dropped in a compact and her toothbrush before
zipping it closed.

She brushed past Helen and went into the attic room, where a larger canvas bag lay half filled atop the quilted bedspread. Helen followed, taking a seat on an over-stuffed chair. "Could I ask you a question, sweetheart?"

"Sure," Nancy said without so much as glancing up.

"Now don't take this the wrong way," Helen began, not sure how to put it. "But I was wondering about you and Max."

Nancy's chin jerked up. "Me and Max Simpson?"

Helen fiddled with a button coming loose from the chair's tufting. "When I saw you across the bridge, talking with him, he seemed pretty, um, passionate."

"Passionate?"

"He cheated on Grace, right?" Helen said and gazed straight into Nancy's flushed face. "His alibi for the night Grace was killed was another woman, and a married one at that. So I couldn't help thinking that maybe you and he—"

"You think I slept with Max?" Nancy interrupted. But instead of answering, she pressed her lips together and forcefully shoved several pairs of socks into her duffel bag.

"Did you?"

"Grandma!"

"Nancy, please," Helen said, getting up from the chair and going over to the bed. "It's important that I know what's going on. If you don't tell me now, I'm sure the sheriff will find out, and he could take it all the wrong way."

Nancy stood stock-still for a moment. Then she dropped onto the bed and sighed. "I didn't sleep with him," she said, shaking her head. "He did drop by the office a few times to see Grace, and he hit on me big-time." She squirmed. "Maybe he asked me out once or twice, but I didn't go."

"Did Grace know?"

"I don't think so," Nancy said. "If she had, she would've fired me long ago. Besides, he had plenty of other women. That's why Grace wouldn't take him back. Well, that and the money."

"What money?" Helen asked, and her heart pounded faster. "Did he steal from her?"

Nancy shrugged. "Honestly, I don't know. Grace just complained about him trying to bleed her dry. But I could tell that she still loved him. I think that's why the divorce wasn't final when she died." She cocked her head. "So is this inquisition done?"

"Inquisition?" Helen feigned offense. "I'm as bad as all that?"

Nancy smiled and approached, kissing the top of her grandmother's head. "You're very curious, that's all," she said. "Curious as a cat."

Then she picked up her bag, hooking its strap across a shoulder. "I'll bring my laptop over tomorrow and hang out with you while I hunt for a new job online. Is that all right?"

Helen stood. "You're welcome here anytime."

She followed her granddaughter downstairs and walked her to the porch. From behind the screens, she stood and watched as Nancy headed up the road. The girl turned once to wave before she went around the bend and was gone.

Chapter 28

THE MORE HELEN thought about Grace Simpson's murder and everything she'd learned so far, the less it all made sense.

After the manuscript had been discovered burning in Alma's trash, she felt more sure than ever that Grace's unpublished tell-all book was not at the heart of the crime but merely a red herring. And it had worked remarkably well, seeing as how Frank Biddle seemed convinced that all clues led to Nancy.

If the perpetrator's goal had been to destroy the manuscript, why wouldn't destruction have been enough? Why kill Grace?

Helen sighed, ignoring the crossword that lay on her lap. She stared out the porch screens, not seeing the green of tree-covered bluffs beyond, concentrating instead on the tangle of ideas running through her head.

Who had known Grace would be meeting with Harold

Faulkner in St. Louis that particular night? Nancy had, of course, and Helen figured everyone at LaVyrle's had found out, since Grace had gone to get her hair done beforehand and had been confronted by the angry mob before she'd left.

But who stood to profit most from her death?

Was it Max? Unless Grace had a long-lost relative, he appeared to be the likely—and only—beneficiary, especially if the rumor was true about Grace not having a will.

What about Harold Faulkner, Grace's publisher? Had there been problems between them that would've made publication of her book simpler with Grace gone?

Then there was that troublemaker, Charlie Bryan, whom Biddle had locked up for allegedly selling stolen goods. Had Charlie gone to Grace's house to rob her, assuming she'd be out for the evening, and been surprised by her return? If so, did that mean the other burglaries might be Charlie's doing as well? It seemed to fit the pattern, Helen thought, noting that Mavis White, Violet Farley, and Mattie Oldbridge had all been away when their homes had been violated. If one of them had come home unexpectedly, would they have been killed?

Helen had known all three were going away, as had the rest of the regulars at LaVyrle's. Mavis had been in the salon to have her hair colored before her daughter's wedding. Violet had come in for a cut and blow-dry before a bridge tournament in Kansas City. Mattie had had her nails done before spending the weekend with her nephew in St. Louis. All three were widows who lived alone. Grace, too, was a single woman on her own. Was that the connection? Was the real motive robbery, only in Grace's case a bungled one?

Why were there no telltale signs of who did it? Helen recalled Sarah Biddle telling her that the sheriff had found no fingerprints at Mattie's house and no signs of forced entry. How had the thief or thieves broken in without actually *breaking* and entering? Had they somehow gotten keys? Did they know enough to wear gloves?

Helen pressed her fingers to her temples.

She felt as confused as ever.

Something about the crimes nagged at the back of her brain, but she couldn't single out what it was. She only seemed to shove the thought further away the harder she tried to retrieve it.

Pushing her puzzle aside, she rose to her sneakered feet and tugged down her pink warm-up jacket. She snatched up her purse and headed out to her gray Chevy, quickly slipping behind the wheel. She drove the few blocks to the beauty shop, pulling against the curb and noticing the CLOSED sign in the window.

Rats, she thought, knowing the salon would stay closed until Tuesday. LaVyrle always took Sunday and Monday off. And what was it Mary had told her after the service? Hadn't she mentioned LaVyrle was working another job on her days off?

Helen had only been listening with half an ear, too busy watching Max Simpson holding onto Nancy's arm. Had Mary mentioned *where* LaVyrle was working part-time?

Just as she was about to pull away from the curb, she

looked up to see a familiar brown-haired girl emerging from the diner.

"Mary!" she called, forgetting her windows were closed.

She pressed a hand on the horn.

The girl looked up, pushing aside the brown curtain of overgrown bangs from her eyes. She waved and smiled.

Helen finally got her windows down and motioned the young woman over. Mary stooped down to peer through the passenger side.

"Hey, Mrs. Evans," she said in her feather-soft voice. "I just finished up lunch. Erma had a special on meat loaf sandwiches, and they're my favorite."

"Yes, they're very good," Helen agreed, leaning over the console. "I had some questions I wanted to ask LaVyrle about Grace Simpson."

"About Grace?" The girl rubbed at her elbows. "Why?"

"You told me Grace was a regular of LaVyrle's."

"Uh-huh."

"Maybe she mentioned something to LaVyrle the day she was killed and LaVyrle forgot because it seemed unimportant at the time," Helen said, throwing out, "perhaps she was meeting with someone that night other than her publisher."

"Oh, I see." Mary nodded her head. The motion knocked her hair into her eyes again. She tried to tuck the strands behind her ears, but they didn't seem to want to stay.

"You said she was working somewhere else on Sundays and Mondays?" Helen prodded. "Can you tell me where?"

Mary looked around her. "I wish I hadn't told you that, Mrs. Evans. LaVyrle doesn't want folks to know. She doesn't want them feeling sorry for her."

"It's important, Mary, please."

Mary's eyes fell to her feet. "She's working at a hardware store in Alton. It's called Ernie's, and it's across from the casino boat downtown."

"Thank you, dear."

The girl's chin lifted. Her eyes blinked. "But don't let on that I told you."

"I won't."

With a wave, Helen was off.

It took her twenty minutes to reach Alton and find the hardware store Mary had described. The place was indeed just across the highway from the *Alton Belle*, and Helen was afraid at first that she might have to use the casino's lot when she could find no parking close by. But then a car rolled out of Ernie's side lot, and she quickly took its place.

Helen told herself to proceed carefully. She didn't want to get Mary in trouble, and she didn't want to put LaVyrle on the spot. Helen had been a client of the Cut 'n' Curl for long enough to know that LaVyrle's customers were the ones who spilled their guts, not the other way around. When it came to her own life, LaVyrle was as tight-lipped as they came.

Helen locked her car door as she left the Chevy, wondering how a mom-and-pop store like Ernie's could stay in business with the monstrous chains and discount places that were its competition nowadays. But she was glad of it, regardless.

Outside the front doors, stacks of wooden planters filled with annuals greeted her. A sticker on the glass door said PUSH and Helen did just that, pausing as she stepped inside.

Several checkout counters sat vacant at the front. A row of carpet cleaners for rent lined a wall, and a station where keys were made occupied a near corner. A static-plagued radio station drifted over her head, though Helen couldn't tell whether the song it played was Sinatra or Patsy Cline.

"Hello?" she called out, hugging her purse to her side. When no one came, she started wandering the product-filled aisles. She finally found a white-haired man in stained gray slacks and matching gray shirt with a nametag. He was poking through a shelf filled with marked-down nuts, bolts, and screws.

"Do you work here?" she asked, only to have him shake his head.

So she moved on.

In the garden section with the rubber hoses and plastic thermometers, she spotted a silver-haired woman carefully inspecting several brands of birdfeeders and a man in the power tool aisle talking with a salesclerk in a baseball cap and a bright red apron. Helen almost walked right past until she heard LaVyrle's voice.

"Look at this model, all right? If it's not the most durable drill kit you ever saw, then I'll be a monkey's uncle."

Helen rounded the corner.

"LaVyrle?"

The familiar voice shut up. The customer didn't look away from the red kit in his hands, but the clerk's shoulders stiffened.

"I'll be back in a minute, hon," she told the man, giving him a pat. "Don't you go anywhere now, ya hear?"

Helen gawked as LaVyrle approached in jeans and sneakers beneath the red apron. Helen had never seen the beautician in anything but skirts and high heels. Even LaVyrle's face wasn't dolled up, and she was minus her telltale blond bouffant. Without her accoutrements, she looked plain and nearly unrecognizable. It was an amazing transformation.

But the scowl on her lips was pure LaVyrle Hunnecker.

Helen smiled awkwardly. "I'm sorry to bother you at work, LaVyrle, but we need to talk."

LaVyrle latched hold of her elbow, dragging her out of the aisle and around the corner with such force that Helen felt strong-armed. She caught her breath as LaVyrle propelled her into an empty aisle between shelves of light fixtures and finally released her.

"What in blazes are ya doin' here, Mrs. E?" she ground out. "How on earth did ya find where I was working, anyway? Did Mary blab? I should wring that girl's neck."

"For heaven's sake," Helen murmured and rubbed her sore arm. "I hope you don't treat all your customers like this, or you won't get much repeat business."

"I'm sorry," LaVyrle apologized, exhaling slowly. "I didn't mean t' hurt you. I was just surprised t' see you here."

"It's okay." Helen bent her elbow then straightened it. "I'll survive."

LaVyrle glanced behind her. "You know, the Walmart in Jerseyville's a lot more convenient—"

"Which is why you're not working there, eh?" Helen remarked. "Though I don't see why you felt the need to hide the fact you've gotten yourself a second job. It's not a crime. A lot of people have to do it to pay the bills."

"I'm not hiding," LaVyrle insisted and crossed her arms. "I just like t' keep my personal life to myself. Is *that* a crime?"

"No." Helen shook her head, feeling like a Nosy Nellie once again.

"You know how the ladies in town are," LaVyrle said. "If they'd have known I was here at Ernie's these past three months, I'd have been the hot topic at the shop instead of who's throwing what party or who's goin' on a vacation." Her pale cheeks blushed. "Gossip's good for business, but I don't wanna be the main event."

"I understand." Helen fiddled with her purse strap. "I know I said this before, but if things are really so bad, you can ask for assistance. It's okay to accept a helping hand."

LaVyrle lifted her eyes. "So you're determined t' make me the church's next charity case, is that it? Think you can sell enough quilts to pay Mary's salary and the rest of the shop's expenses? How about taking care of my rent, too, and making sure my mom's got enough in the bank for her and Justin. . . ."

She caught herself, not saying more. Beneath the red apron, her chest rapidly rose and fell. "Never mind," she said, waving Helen off. "I can take care of what's mine. I'll do whatever I have to t' hold my own."

"Who is Justin?" Helen couldn't stop herself from asking. "Was that the boy in the picture that fell out of your drawer?"

LaVyrle gave her a hard look. "Excuse me if I don't want my family t' be the subject of conversation at your next bridge game."

Helen was taken aback. "Do I seem as callous as that?"

"I don't need my laundry aired out for all of River Bend t' see, you got that?"

Helen couldn't speak.

"It's not just you." LaVyrle sniffed. "I know how folks talk. I know their bad habits and whatever good ones they've got, what their husbands eat for dinner, whose kids have diaper rash, what they got for Christmas."

"I guess we do tend to talk when someone's willing to listen," Helen remarked with a frown. She dared to touch LaVyrle's arm and felt it tremble. "I don't want you to be afraid to come to me if you feel desperate or if your son needs anything—"

"Justin's fine." LaVyrle shrugged off her touch. "My mom's been takin' care of him for me ever since his daddy took off when he was born. He stays with her in Godfrey." She lifted her chin, and her unmade-up face looked so vulnerable that it nearly broke Helen's heart. "I got things under control like I always do. So you can leave Ernie's knowing you did your good deed for the day, all right? I got work to do, besides."

"Wait! I didn't even ask you about Grace," Helen tried to say, but LaVyrle walked away before she finished.

Helen didn't have the guts to chase LaVyrle down. Besides, her mind twisted and turned with all the things LaVyrle had told her, pieces of a woman's life that had remained hidden in shadow. How could she have felt like she'd known the beautician so well when she'd hardly known her at all?

Helen left Ernie's Hardware with a sad knot in her chest. She drove back to River Bend in silence, no more sure of anything or anyone than when she'd left.

Chapter 29

HELEN TURNED OFF the highway and rolled into River Bend. Preoccupied with her thoughts, she barely gave the old lighthouse with its bright red roof a cursory glance as she passed it by. As she entered the town proper, she hardly noticed Serenity Garden, with its newly planted zinnias, snapdragons, and daisies. A woman with a watering can straightened up from the flowerbeds and lifted a hand to wave, but Helen caught the motion too late from the corner of her eye, so she tucked her chin down and drove on.

What am I missing? Helen kept asking herself as she headed down Main Street toward home. Why did it seem that the more she dug for answers, the more questions she turned up?

She sensed that everything she needed was there, stored away in her head. If only she could dip in her hand

and snatch out that one piece tying the odds and ends together.

Like an elusive word in a crossword, it would come to her in time. Helen only hoped that she could wait.

When she reached the downtown, Helen slowed to a snail's pace, noticing a small commotion in front of the sheriff's office. Several people stood on the sidewalk, and there were more across the street outside the diner, watching as Biddle helped a passenger out of his squad car. Helen recognized the woman—Hilary Dell, who owned the stationery store and who was a substitute for Helen's bridge group. The two quickly disappeared into the sheriff's office, and the rubberneckers began to disperse.

She saw Agnes March looking on from in front of her antiques store, and Helen rolled down a window, calling out, "What's going on?"

"Hey, there, Helen," Agnes said, fingering the pearls at her throat as she leaned into the window. "You're just getting back to town, are you?"

"I've been in Alton."

"Then you've missed all the excitement." Agnes's weathered face grew animated. "There's been another burglary."

"What?"

"This time it was at Hilary Dell's," Agnes told her and wrinkled her nose. "She'd been away for one night and returned this morning to find her place ransacked. She'd put up a camera over her back door after Mattie's place was broken into, so they know who did it."

"They do?"

Agnes nodded. "It was Charlie Bryan. Hilary said the image was kind of iffy, but there was no doubt in her mind."

"Charlie Bryan," Helen repeated, wondering how that was possible. Hadn't the sheriff put him in lockup overnight? How on earth could he be two places at once?

"Been nice chatting, Helen," Agnes said and smiled. "But I'd better get back to the store."

"Yes, of course."

A horn honked behind her, and Helen moved forward enough to slip into a vacant parking spot on the street.

She grabbed her bag and hurried to the door of Biddle's office. With a gulp of air, she squared her shoulders and marched inside.

"Let me get the image on the screen so we can get a good look at it," Biddle was saying as he fiddled with a computer on his desk, swiveling it around so Hilary Dell could see the monitor from the chair in which she sat.

When Helen shut the door behind her with a click, the sheriff glanced up. Hilary's head swiveled. Her face looked puffy and very upset.

"Helen!" Hilary cried out, seeming happy to see her.

"Mrs. Evans," the sheriff said, far less pleased by the intrusion. "What are you doing here?"

"I need to talk to you about the murder," Helen said as she approached his desk.

"Well, can it wait?" Biddle asked. "I'm in the middle of something here."

"My dear friend," Helen cooed and went over to Hilary. She settled on the chair beside her. "Are you all right?"

The other woman nodded. "I'm okay, Helen, just shaken up a bit."

The sheriff cleared his throat. "Like I was saying, ma'am, Mrs. Dell and I are in the middle of something."

Helen gestured at the computer screen. "Please, go on," she told him. "I'll sit here quiet as a mouse. You don't mind, Hilary, do you?"

Her friend shook her head. "Not a bit."

Biddle grumbled as he fed a DVD into the system. Pretty soon, black-and-white images filled the monitor.

The picture looked crisp enough to Helen. She could see the back door and stoop of Hilary's house, as well as part of the driveway.

"My goodness," she remarked, "wherever did you get such a thing? Did you have to call a security company?"

"Would you believe I ordered it online?" Hilary replied. "It's rather like the monitor my daughter used for her kids, only it's meant for outdoors and has night vision and records on a DVR. My son-in-law set it up the day after Mattie got robbed. I wouldn't have felt safe otherwise."

"Incredible," Helen murmured, thinking you could order just about anything these days and have it delivered right to your door.

"I can send you a link if you're interested," Hilary said, only to have Biddle clear his throat again loudly.

"Ladies," he grumbled.

"Sorry," Helen said and made a motion of zipping her lips.

She watched as the sheriff fast-forwarded to a certain time and date stamp on the screen. Then she heard Hilary's sharp intake of breath as a shadowy figure hovered on the periphery.

"This is from last night at 11:48," Biddle told them, and Helen guessed that was why things looked such a weird shade of green. It must have been the night vision.

"There he is," Hilary yelped, pointing at the screen. "There's the thief!"

Helen squinted, trying to focus on the person in question. The camera must have been perched above the garage door, as it caught the back of the intruder as he hurried across the driveway. She hadn't even seen a face. Within moments, the thief had disappeared into the house.

"He had a key?" Helen asked.

"He must have," Hilary moaned. "Though I don't know how he would have gotten it."

"Let's move on, shall we?" Biddle remarked. He tapped a few keys and fast-forwarded a total of fifteen minutes so they could watch the figure emerge.

The sheriff tapped a key and froze the screen. "This is the best we've got," he said and looked at Hilary. "You still think that's Charlie Bryan?"

"Yes, yes, it's him!" Hilary replied, sounding so sure. "Who else could it be?"

Helen cocked her head, studying the image, but she couldn't make out the features distinctly enough to be convinced.

What she saw was someone of average height wearing dark jeans and a baseball cap pulled low enough to disguise half the face. But there was something off, something that didn't feel right. Maybe it was the shape of the jaw or the size of the feet. Charlie wasn't a large boy, to be sure, but the sneakers looked about the size of Nancy's.

"Are you sure that's Charlie, Sheriff?" Helen asked, but Frank Biddle didn't seem to hear her. She glanced at the door to lockup. "But Charlie couldn't have—" she started to say, only Biddle talked right over her comment.

"If you want to hang around, Mrs. Dell, I'll put you in the break room to fill out some paperwork. Then I can drive you home."

"Yes, I can stay," Hilary told him. She looked at Helen as she picked up her purse and stood. "You should order a camera, too, hon. Otherwise, you'll never know what's going on while you're gone."

"I'll think about it," Helen told her.

Biddle rounded up the paperwork from his desk. He arched his eyebrows at Helen. "So you're hanging around, too."

"I'll be right here when you finish with Hilary."

"I can't wait."

Helen didn't let his sarcasm get to her. What she needed to discuss with him was far too important, and it seemed even more so after she'd viewed Hilary's video. How could the sheriff believe the person in the video was

Charlie? Unless he'd released the boy before midnight, it couldn't possibly be him.

Ten minutes later, the sheriff returned. He sat down on the edge of his desk, facing Helen. Before she could open her mouth, he raised his hand.

"I know what you're going to say."

"You do?"

"She's wrong," he announced and scratched his jaw. "That wasn't Charlie."

Helen let out a held breath. "Oh, Sheriff, I'm so relieved to hear you say so. I'd hate for the boy to get in even more trouble when he's been telling the truth all along."

Biddle nodded.

"So he's still locked up?"

"Since yesterday."

"Hilary doesn't know?" Helen asked.

"Not yet, ma'am," Biddle told her, rubbing tired eyes. "Maybe Sarah didn't open her mouth so wide this time after all."

"Maybe not," Helen agreed.

"Someone clearly wants to pin the burglaries on Charlie," he said, and his gaze went to the frozen image on the computer screen, "enough to dress like the kid and make full use of his bad rep. Only this time, they screwed up. Charlie has an alibi."

"He didn't break into Hilary's," Helen said, just to be clear.

"No."

"And he wasn't lying when he told you he didn't steal that cigarette case from Mattie's," she added. "Could be he really did find it behind her house."

"Yep." Biddle drew in a sharp breath.

"So he probably didn't kill Grace Simpson either," Helen said.

"Nope," Biddle grunted and shut off the computer. He tugged a set of keys from his belt and singled out one.

"You're going to release him?"

"I am."

Helen nodded. "Good. And when you're done with Charlie and with Hilary, too, I need you to do something for me as well."

The sheriff's hangdog face looked up. "What's that?"

"I need you to get a search warrant," she said.

"You need me to . . . what?"

"If we can just check out a feeling I have, I think we can put an end to this whole matter once and for all."

"The whole matter being . . . ?"

"The burglaries," Helen told him, clutching her purse in her lap, "and the murder of Grace Simpson. I believe I know the culprit."

"Ma'am, I can't ask a judge for a warrant to search someone's house on your hunch. I've got to have probable cause," he explained, staring at her as though she'd gone stark raving mad.

"Then go for a drive with me after you've delivered Hilary home," she said. "Maybe you'll see something that will give you cause enough."

Biddle squinted at her. "And just where are we going to go?"

Helen met his eyes. "I'll let you know when we get there."

Chapter 30

THE HOUSE SAT at the dead end of Springfield Avenue. To venture further meant ending up in a tangle of trees and a dried-up bed of rocks, which had once lined a flowing creek until the river had run low for too many years.

Helen hadn't explained where she'd wanted to go until Biddle had gotten into her car and they'd been well on their way. When she'd told him, he'd balked.

"You think she's the perp?"

"I do."

"You honestly believe that she could have—"

"Yes, Sheriff," Helen said sadly, "I'm afraid I do."

There was no curb or even a dirt driveway. In this spot where Springfield dead ended, there was only a graveled circle so that misguided cars could turn around. It was on the circle that Helen finally parked.

For a long moment, the pair of them stared up at the house. It sat alone, looking neglected. Helen wasn't certain why no one else had ever built at this tip of Springfield; then again, perhaps she did realize why after all.

As she got out of the car and stepped onto the uneven stone path leading up to the door, she gazed around her at the encircling woods. Cicadas, crickets, and a host of other unseen insects noisily hummed; the odd music they created seemed louder here than nearer to town. Otherwise, an unnatural hush pervaded the area so that the slam of the passenger door as Biddle got out seemed unduly sharp, so much so that Helen jumped.

"You all right, Mrs. Evans?"

She settled the straps of her purse into place and steadied herself. "Yes, Sheriff," she told him, "I'm fine."

Could be her sudden nerves were due to the stretch of tree boughs above them that seemed to cut off sky and sunlight. Or maybe it had to do with the fact that not a single other rooftop could be seen from where she stood, which gave the impression that they'd driven well into the country.

"Ma'am?"

Biddle touched her arm and she walked ahead with him, stumbling once or twice on the uneven stones. Even still, she refused the hand he offered.

They went up half a dozen steps to a porch littered with fallen leaves and dirt. The house desperately needed a new coat of paint and a set of new shutters. Though a mat at the door bid them welcome, Helen felt anything but.

The sheriff paused at the door, turning to give her an uncertain look. "I know you told me why you wanted to come here, Mrs. Evans, but it seems far-fetched that—"

"This is the house of a killer?" Helen said. "I hope I'm wrong, Sheriff. In fact, I'd love to be. But I don't think I am."

He reached for the doorbell and rang it once, then twice. Helen didn't stop him even though she knew there was no one home.

"Oh, for goodness' sake," she said and tried the knob. If there was any door in town still left unlocked, it would be this one. Why would a thief have to worry about being robbed?

"Ma'am, you can't just bust in," Biddle protested as Helen pushed the front door wide.

"Is that a cry for help I hear?" she said, cocking her ear.

"What cry?"

"Yes, I'm sure it was," Helen fibbed, and her heart raced. She was afraid as much of the lie she'd just told as she was of what they might find. "C'mon, Sheriff, isn't it your duty to check things out if someone might be hurt?"

"Ma'am, this doesn't feel right," he grumbled, but Helen was already inside.

The house was dim, but enough sunlight filtered through the place for Helen to make out the faded floral wallpaper and dull wood floor beneath their feet.

Biddle's voice broke through her thoughts. "There's no one here, is there? The place is quiet as a library."

"You can always wait outside," she told him and took in a deep breath.

The air smelled decidedly musty, but there was another scent that lingered. Helen recalled the odor she'd detected at Grace Simpson's house, one that had seemed familiar somehow, though at the time she'd been unable

to pinpoint why that was. Mattie Oldbridge had mentioned a weird scent at her place after she'd gotten home
from her nephew's. Helen had a feeling that they were one
and the same.

She realized then what that smell had reminded her
of: the beauty shop.

"This is breaking and entering," the sheriff said as he
followed her from one room to the next.

"But we didn't break anything," Helen reminded him,
taking in the spare furnishings. "The door was unlocked."

"We weren't invited in—"

"We heard a scream."

"No, we didn't."

"Maybe you didn't hear the cry for help," Helen insisted, "but I certainly did. I just wish it hadn't taken me
so darned long to listen."

The cry she'd heard had been real enough, though it
had been silent, not loud. If only Helen had recognized
it before things had gotten so bad that they'd pushed the
back of someone she'd known and liked flat against the
wall.

She spotted a picture frame on the fireplace mantel
beside a Mason jar filled with grimy plastic flowers. The
photograph showed a woman and a baby.

"Justin," Helen said, knowing who the baby was.

*I can take care of what's mine. I'll do whatever I have
to t' hold my own.*

She hadn't realized she'd actually uttered the words
until the sheriff asked, "You say something, ma'am?"

"Just thinking out loud," she told him.

Without touching anything, Helen left the room. She didn't even grip the banister as she ascended the stairs.

When she reached the bedroom, she stood in the doorway at first.

The bed was covered in a quilt, its patches faded. The walls might have been white once, but now they were the color of an eggshell, the plaster cracked and yellowed. There was another photograph of a boy tucked into the frame of a bureau mirror. On the dresser top was something else as revealing: a Styrofoam head upon which perched a blond wig combed into a bouffant.

"I think I will go outside, ma'am," Sheriff Biddle said from behind her. "I don't know what you're up to exactly, but I don't think I can be a part of this. And if I knew what was good for me, I'd drag you out as well."

Helen nodded and soon heard the clunk of his boots on the stairs.

She went into the bathroom and caught her reflection in the mirror above the stained porcelain sink. She didn't have to open up the medicine cabinet. She knew it would be filled with all the things a beautician would require for herself: beauty products, nail polishes, and lotions.

An old fashioned helmet hair dryer sat in its case on the floor. A soggy pair of panty hose hung over the shower affixed to the claw-footed tub. A shuttered pantry, half opened, revealed folded towels and extra rolls of toilet paper. A wicker hamper stood against the wall, its lid missing so that Helen could easily peer inside.

Her heart thumped faster.

Was it possible that the thief had known where to

find so many things because it was where she hid her things, too?

Helen looked at the doorway behind her, making sure the sheriff hadn't come back up without her hearing. But she was alone.

She sucked in a breath and dipped a hand into the wicker basket, reaching past assorted bits of laundry to the bottom. Just as she'd hoped, her hand encountered something odd. It was a pillowcase tied in a knot. When she picked it up, its contents jingled. Without thinking too much about what she was doing, she sat down on the toilet seat and put the makeshift bag in her lap.

Frowning so her thick eyebrows sat low over her eyes, she worked the knot out and opened the pillowcase. The box that rattled within proclaimed it to contain "bobby pins," though it felt far too heavy to hold only that.

Helen slid a fingernail under the lid and popped open the box to reveal a host of keys, a dozen at least. Each had a name taped to it. "Farley," one label read, and another, "White." Still more were tagged "Oldbridge," "Dell," "Wiggins," and "Simpson." To her distress, Helen even found one marked "Evans."

"Good God," Helen breathed. Had all of them been targets? Might she herself have been next?

She put the keys back in the box and felt around inside the pillowcase for whatever remained. She pulled out a batch of tickets neatly rubber-banded together. Helen held them far enough away to read: East Alton Pawn, St. Charles Pawn, Kinloch, Wellston, Belleville, and Granite City.

Out-of-the-way spots, all of them.

Mattie's candlesticks from Mexico, Violet's pearls from Japan, Mavis's emerald earrings . . . Helen thought of those treasures and others, stolen and sold by the thief.

Charlie Bryan had doubtless been telling the sheriff the truth when he'd said he'd found that cigarette case. And if he hadn't been put in lockup because he'd sold the piece to a flea market vendor in Grafton, he would have been without an alibi, and the blame for Hilary Dell's burglary would most certainly have been placed on him.

I'll do whatever I have to t' hold my own.

The words wouldn't let her go. They played over and over in Helen's head.

I know how folks talk. I know their bad habits and whatever good ones they've got, what their husbands eat for dinner, whose kids have diaper rash, what they got for Christmas.

Helen hadn't wanted to believe it, but everything fit.

She'd found the missing piece she'd been looking for—the keys and pawnshop tickets hidden in the clothes hamper—and now everything snapped into place.

Only Helen felt as if she'd lost a battle instead of winning one.

Sadly, she stuffed the box of keys and pawn tickets back into the pillowcase. She knew she couldn't take it to the sheriff. She was snooping inside a house without any kind of legal authority, making everything she'd found worthless. Sheriff Biddle would have to discover this evidence on his own.

With a sigh, she got up off the toilet seat.

"What the hell's going on here?" a voice that was not Frank Biddle's said from the doorway.

Helen lifted downcast eyes, catching a glimpse of sneakers, then jeans, and her gaze traveled upward to meet LaVyrle's furious eyes. Usually so quick with a comeback, Helen drew a blank. She watched LaVyrle's stare fall on the pillowcase, and Helen swallowed hard. Talk about getting caught red-handed.

Chapter 31

"I SAW YOUR car out front, but I never imagined you'd be inside my house, going through my things." LaVyrle's gaze didn't waver from the balled-up pillowcase in Helen's hands. "You got something that's mine, Mrs. E. So why don't you just hand it over t' me now?"

Helen backed away from the toilet but merely ended up bumping against the sink. "I thought you were at work," she said, never having imagined LaVyrle would return before five o'clock when the hardware store closed.

LaVyrle plucked off her baseball cap, revealing closely cropped brown hair. "I got a sense you were up t' something," she said. "I told my boss Justin was sick and I had t' leave." She shook her head. "I wish I'd been wrong."

"Me, too," Helen whispered.

LaVyrle reached a hand out, gesturing with pink-tipped fingers. "Give that back, Mrs. E. Don't make me hurt you."

Hurt her? Like she'd hurt Grace Simpson? Murder was a powerful kind of pain, wasn't it?

"Oh, LaVyrle," Helen sighed. Her heart felt broken. "I didn't want to believe it was true. I did everything to convince myself otherwise. But in the end, it was the only answer that made sense."

LaVyrle gave up on getting Helen to relinquish the pillowcase. She braced her hands against the doorjamb instead. "What exactly d'you think you know?"

Helen patted the pillowcase. "You're the serial burglar who stole from Mavis White, Violet Farley, Mattie Oldbridge, and Hilary Dell. I'm guessing you meant to rob from Grace Simpson, only she returned home and surprised you."

LaVyrle laughed, but she didn't move. She had Helen effectively trapped, and she knew it. "You've got a wild imagination, Mrs. E. But then you always were a lively old broad. I think that's why I liked you best. Now hand over my stuff."

Helen didn't relinquish the bag. She maneuvered around the sink and pressed her back to the tiled wall. "We trusted you," she said. "We all left our purses with you when we went to get shampooed. You had ten minutes at least to take out our keys and find the one you wanted."

Dark eyebrows arched. "You think I stole keys from my clients? Don't you figure someone would've noticed?"

"You didn't steal them exactly." Helen shook her head, thinking of Nancy's makeover and rummaging through LaVyrle's drawer, looking for Kleenex. "The blocks of wax," she said and met LaVyrle's angry stare. "You used the paraffin wax meant for manicures to make impressions of the keys. Then you used that as a mold."

"Give me a break," LaVyrle said with a snort. She pushed away from the doorjamb and grabbed a towel bar. "And who'd make me a key from a wax impression?"

"You," Helen answered, wishing her legs didn't feel so unsteady. "The hardware store has the equipment for making keys. I saw it myself. It wouldn't be hard to find a close match and copy the notches if you knew how. Even if you had to use a locksmith's file and do it by hand."

"You think I did all that?" LaVyrle rattled the towel bar, which nearly came out of the wall.

"I know you did."

LaVyrle tapped her chin. "And just when do you think I had time t' go breakin' into people's houses? I work two jobs, as you managed to find out."

"You're the one who told me the answer to that, LaVyrle," Helen said. "You know more about the women in this town than anyone. Who lives alone, who's leaving town." Helen paused. The cold from the tile seeped through her clothing, and she shivered. "You'd probably even heard about favorite pieces of jewelry, treasured ornaments, cash. You even knew where things were hidden. People told you their secrets, and you took advantage of that." Helen wet her lips. "Using keys you made yourself, well, you didn't even have to break in. You let yourself inside like you belonged."

"No one can prove anything." LaVyrle rattled the towel bar again. "No one's gonna believe you, Mrs. E, not without evidence. I heard from Sarah Biddle herself that the sheriff never found a single fingerprint."

"The plastic gloves," Helen said and closed her eyes, picturing all the times she'd seen LaVyrle with them on her hands. Every time she gave a perm or colored hair. She had boxes of them, the kind you could just toss away after you'd used them. Helen opened her eyes and sighed. "You always wore disposable gloves so you wouldn't leave behind your prints."

LaVyrle smiled. "You figure I'm as smart as that?"

Helen nodded. "I always did."

"You can't show what you found t' the sheriff," LaVyrle said. "I've seen enough cop shows to know that what you're doin' is illegal. In fact, I should call the sheriff and have you arrested."

"Yes, call him," Helen told her. "The sheriff isn't stupid. He'll put all the pieces together soon enough. He already knows that Charlie Bryan isn't the thief." Helen paused as LaVyrle's eyes narrowed. "Didn't you know Hilary Dell had a surveillance camera? You were caught in the act."

LaVyrle's mouth tightened. "You couldn't understand why I did what I did. Not in a million years."

"I know you're in financial trouble."

"Financial trouble? Is that what you call it?" LaVyrle made a noise of disgust. "You and your widow friends, you're all sittin' so pretty. You got your big fat nest eggs to roost on what with your husbands gone and everything you own. It's not your kind fighting like hell t' survive. Your old man didn't run off and leave you with an empty pocketbook and a kid. He didn't leave you with bills and rent and a business to support. You don't know what it feels like to get sucked under."

"That doesn't give you the right to steal," Helen told her, "or to kill. Why'd you do it? Why'd you kill Grace?"

For the first time, LaVyrle's face showed real fear. "It was an accident," she said in a hoarse whisper. "It wasn't supposed to go down like that."

"You broke into her place, thinking she'd be gone for hours. But she wasn't. She forgot the manuscript, so she had to turn around and go home." Keep talking, Helen's mind instructed. Keep talking and maybe you'll talk your way right out of this. She didn't want to believe LaVyrle would really hurt her. She couldn't. "You were trapped, and Grace found you. You panicked and picked up the bat. Then you hit her and took the manuscript. You knew she'd intended to meet her publisher. You took it so you could throw suspicion on someone else, and that someone else ended up being Nancy."

The snap of the towel bar being wrenched out of the wall cut off further words.

Helen's knees shook.

"I'm sorry, Mrs. E. I really am," LaVyrle said, and she truly looked sad. "But sometimes ya just don't have a choice." She took a step toward Helen and raised the metal bar above her head.

Helen squished her eyes closed and braced for a blow.

Then she heard a grunt, a strangled cry, the clatter of the bar hitting the tiled floor, and the sheriff's deep voice.

"It's all right, Mrs. Evans," he said. "You can open your eyes."

Slowly, she let her lids flutter up.

Frank Biddle stood inside the pink-tiled bathroom. He had LaVyrle pinned against the far wall, her face turned away from Helen. With a snap of metal on metal, he cuffed her hands behind her back.

"My God, Sheriff"—Helen released the breath she'd been holding—"whatever in the world took you so long?"

At that point, her shaky knees gave out and, without a hint of grace, she slid to the floor.

Chapter 32

HELEN SAT IN a wicker rocker, gently moving to and fro. Amber filled her lap entirely, and her fingers stroked his yellow fur. The cat rumbled beneath her touch and closed his eyes, perfectly contented. She could swear his pink-gummed mouth was smiling as he kneaded his paws on her thighs. Every now and then his claws pricked through her warm-up pants, and Helen would carefully disentangle them from the fabric, not missing a beat as she continued petting him with her other hand.

A breeze pressed through the screens, bringing with it the familiar smells of cut grass and a tinge of goldenrod, the latter no doubt contributing to the sporadic sneezes she heard coming from nearby porches.

An occasional car crawled past, its tires grinding over gravel. She could hear a dog barking in the distance and the faint hum of cicadas. Otherwise it was blissfully still.

Helen drew in a deep breath.

The town seemed to have settled back to its usual slow pace after all the recent hullabaloo over Grace's death and the arrest of poor LaVyrle.

"If only she'd asked for help," Helen said aloud, and Amber pricked up his ears. She scratched between them, and his purring grew louder. "If only I'd known she was so desperate."

But LaVyrle hadn't been the type to ask. She hadn't wanted anyone to realize the trouble she'd been in. She was too strong, too proud. So she'd stolen from her clients instead.

"And look where that got her," Helen murmured, shaking her head. "A cell at the Jersey County Jail."

The screen door snapped open and shut, and Helen looked up with a start. She half rose from the rocker, so that Amber spilled from her lap.

"Sorry, Grandma," Nancy said, taking a hesitant step in. "I didn't mean to startle you. I hope I'm not interrupting?"

Helen brushed yellow fur off her pants, watching Amber as he flipped his tail into the air and stomped away. "No, honey, you're not interrupting," she said. "I was just thinking is all."

"Were you on the phone?" Nancy looked around her. "I heard you talking."

Helen laughed. "Yes, to myself. Like a crazy old woman, huh?"

The girl's slender face relaxed. Her bright blue eyes crinkled. She came toward Helen and gave her a bear hug. "Like someone with a lot on her mind," she said into

Helen's ear before she drew away. "I still can't believe what happened. That LaVyrle did all those horrible things."

Helen could hardly believe it either. "It's an awful world we live in that makes a woman resort to breaking the law to keep her home and family. Now her son will grow up without his mother."

"But he already was," Nancy said. "His grandmother's raising him."

"LaVyrle tried to do her best—"

"No, she didn't. She was a thief and she committed murder," Nancy reminded Helen. "No one made her do any of that. She doesn't deserve your sympathy."

"Maybe not," Helen said, but she couldn't help feeling sorry for LaVyrle nonetheless. She believed that LaVyrle hadn't meant to hurt anyone, that LaVyrle had killed Grace impulsively, not with malice. She wanted to believe, too, that LaVyrle would never have hurt her, that she had enough goodness left inside her that she would have put the towel bar down if given the chance.

And still, Helen was glad that Sheriff Biddle had stepped in when he had. Thank goodness she'd taken him along even if he hadn't approved of her means of investigating. "Don't ever," he'd told her sternly after, "do anything like that again."

"Come sit," Nancy said and tugged her hand, guiding Helen over to the sofa and settling down side by side. "Did the sheriff say what's going to happen?"

"She'll be charged with involuntary manslaughter in Grace's death and at least five counts of burglary, including the theft of the manuscript from Grace." Helen stopped, and tears sprang to her eyes. "To think LaVyrle would have let you go to jail for the murder, and she would have let Charlie Bryan take the heat for everything else."

"But it all worked out, didn't it?" Nancy said and patted her knee. "I'm okay, and Charlie's free to jack the mayor's car again."

Helen smiled weakly.

"It's not your fault, Grandma," Nancy whispered, laying her head on Helen's shoulder. "You're not responsible for LaVyrle's troubles."

"You're right, I know." Helen sniffed, brushing away her tears. "Still, if I hadn't been so nosy—"

"Then I'd be locked up in Jersey County and not LaVyrle. You wouldn't want that, would you?"

"No," Helen said firmly. "No, I wouldn't."

The pretty face that stared at her so solemnly made Helen recall an old photograph she had, of herself when she was Nancy's age, and she felt almost as if she was talking to her younger self.

For a moment, they didn't speak; they simply sat side by side.

"Thanks for believing in me," Nancy whispered, "even when no one else in town did."

"How could I not? You've never lied to me before," Helen said, then paused. "At least not that I know about."

Nancy laughed, and Helen realized it was the first time she'd heard the sound since the whole mess with Grace had started.

"So, what are your plans?" she asked her granddaughter. "Will you stick around?"

Nancy lifted her head from Helen's shoulder. She bit her lip, as if afraid her decision might not sit well with her grandmother. "I've been thinking—"

"Yes?"

"I think I might go back to school," Nancy confessed. "I'd like to get my master's in social work. Does that sound okay to you?"

"Does that sound okay?" Helen pulled back. "It sounds fantastic."

Nancy shrugged. "Maybe someday I can help someone like LaVyrle so she can make better choices before it's too late.

"I like that idea."

"You do?"

"I like it very much."

Nancy grinned.

"There's just one thing," Helen started to say, and Nancy looked worried.

"What is it?"

"Just that I'll miss you," Helen admitted, at which point Nancy flung her arms around Helen's shoulders and buried her face in the crook of her neck.

"Oh, Grandma, I'll miss you, too," she said.

AFTER NANCY LEFT, teary-eyed but happy, Helen made sure the shoelaces on her sneakers were securely tied. She patted her jacket pocket, checking for the good-bye gift Nancy had given her, then she set out on her daily walk.

The sun shone down brightly, showering her in its warmth. She kept her gaze straight ahead, glancing down only now and then to avoid bigger cracks in the sidewalk or an errant pile of doggy-do that had somehow missed the grass.

She slowed her steps when she reached the center of downtown, and she found her eyes drawn across the street.

The plate-glass window with the purple script advertising LaVyrle's Cut 'n' Curl winked back at her. A CLOSED sign dangled from the door, causing a knot in Helen's chest. She wondered if that sign would ever again read OPEN.

A shadow crossed her face, blotting out the sun, and Helen turned to see Frank Biddle blocking her path.

"Hi, Sheriff," she said.

He nodded, replying with a clipped, "Ma'am." He stood with thumbs hooked into his gun belt, the overhang of his belly straining the buttons on his shirt. He tipped his hat so it sat well back on his head. "I thought you'd appreciate hearing a bit of good news about Grace Simpson. That is"—he wrinkled his brow—"if Sarah hasn't told you already."

"What about Grace?" she asked.

"It appears that the woman had a will," Biddle said, "a handwritten one, all perfectly legal."

"Is that right?"

"Yep."

"Did Max get everything?" Helen said, hoping that wasn't the case. The man didn't deserve a bloody penny.

"Apparently, she left all her worldly goods to a half dozen charities," Biddle told her, grinning. "Max Simpson's protesting, of course."

"What a weasel." Helen scoffed. "It is nice to know Grace had a soft spot in her heart after all."

"Or else she just wanted to make sure that poor excuse for a husband didn't get his hands on her money," the sheriff suggested.

"Somehow *that* sounds more like her," Helen said and looked past the sheriff, suddenly impatient to resume her walk.

"Um, ma'am?"

"Yes, Sheriff?" Helen felt the breeze tug at her gray curls. Though she was still half a mile at least from the Mississippi, the wind coming off the river teased her nose with its ripe, muddy smell.

He cleared his throat and ran a finger under his collar. "I, um . . . well, I just wanted to tell you that I'm sorry for what I put you through, and I appreciate what you did."

"You do?" She cocked her head and raised a hand above her eyes to block out the sun peeking over Biddle's shoulder. "I thought you didn't like me poking my nose where it didn't belong?"

"Well, I don't, of course," he told her, fumbling to find the words. "But maybe sometimes the end does justify the means."

Helen grinned. "Even when that means involves being a busybody?"

"I, um, don't know that I'd put it that way," he muttered. "I'm just glad that it's over."

He tugged the beak of his hat back over his brow. "Except that it isn't," he said, "not entirely."

"Oh?" Helen's pulse thumped a little bit faster. "Why's that?"

"You don't happen to know anything about that missing flash drive, do you?" he asked, watching her far too closely. "Grace Simpson's publisher has been breathing down my neck about it since LaVyrle made toast of the physical manuscript. I know Nancy said she gave it back to her boss, but I never found it with any of Grace's possessions."

"Hmm," Helen murmured.

"You don't know if your granddaughter still has it, by chance?"

"I'm sorry, Sheriff, but she doesn't," Helen told him, putting her hands in her pockets. "I guess Mr. Faulkner won't be publishing Grace's book after all. Such a pity."

"Yeah, a pity," Biddle echoed, but Helen caught his dry smile.

She gave a wave and took off, pumping her arms as she walked, not stopping again until she reached the river. Instead of stopping at the edge of town where a clipped field of grass met the River Road, Helen looked both ways, then dashed across the double lanes of asphalt. She didn't pause until she safely reached the bicycle path on the opposite side.

Then she stepped over the guardrail and carefully picked her way down the rocky incline until she stood just above where the brown waters sloshed and slapped at the waterline.

She reached in her pocket, withdrawing a small piece of plastic no bigger than her thumb. With a grunt, she tossed it unceremoniously into the river, as far as she could throw.

"I didn't lie," she whispered to herself. "Nancy really didn't have it."

Her granddaughter had given her the flash drive before she'd taken off, telling her, "You'll know what to do with it, Grandma. Whatever you think is best."

And that was exactly what Helen had done.

Read on for a sneak peek at the next
River Road Mystery
by Susan McBride

NOT A CHANCE IN HELEN

Available September 30th
from Witness Impulse!

Prologue

THE CAB PULLED up in front of the turreted Victorian mansion, and Eleanora Duncan emerged from the back-seat. She plucked cash from her wallet to press through the open window to pay the driver. As quickly as she snatched her hand away, the taxi rolled off, leaving her standing in a cloud of exhaust fumes.

She coughed, waving a gloved hand before her, thinking that between good old pollution and the smoke-filled committee meetings she was forever attending her poor lungs wouldn't last to blow out eighty-one candles on her birthday cake.

She hobbled up the porch steps, pulling off her gloves and stuffing them into her purse. As she reached the front door, she found it ajar.

Heavens to Betsy! She'd only been away for an hour to take her seat on the county hospital board. Had Zelma lost her mind? Eleanora could hardly believe her longtime housekeeper would leave the house accessible to any common thief.

Or worse still, she mused, what if the cat had gotten out?

As if on cue, Lady Godiva's whiskered face peered around the jamb. Before Eleanora could shove the cat back inside, the feline slipped through the doorway. She brushed past Eleanora's ankles and took off without a moment's hesitation.

"Lady!" she called to her precious baby. "Sweetheart, come back here this minute!" She frowned, watching her prized Persian scoot down the porch steps toward the street.

"Bad girl!" Eleanora scolded in a voice two octaves higher than normal. "You know you're not allowed to roam the neighborhood." She pressed blue-veined hands together, thinking of the things her baby could pick up outdoors: the ticks, the fleas, a dirty tom's wanton interest.

"Zelma!" she hollered as she hurried through the door and ducked her head into the foyer. "Zelma? Where the devil are you?"

Damned if the woman wasn't deaf as well as blind, she thought of the housekeeper who'd been with her longer than her husband and son, both of whom had passed two years before, God rest their souls.

Well, Eleanora couldn't wait for Zelma to appear. She turned around and caught sight of Lady Godiva there on the pebble stone path, sniffing at the bordering begonias. "Lady!" she called out again and hooked her purse on the doorknob. Her low heels tapped on the porch floor as she made her way after the cat, her arthritic hips slowing her gait.

She was but a few yards away when the copper-hued Persian lifted her head, tail twitching. Eleanora reached out her arms, smiling hesitantly.

"Come here, precious. Come to Mommy."

She was almost near enough to bend and scoop up Lady when a butterfly swooped down from the sky, fluttering enticingly, and the cat plunged off the curb and into the road.

"Lady Godiva, no!" Eleanora frantically scanned the street right and left, sighing when she saw no traffic. "Please, come back, pretty girl. Oh, for Pete's sake."

By then, she was breathing hard, her silk blouse uncomfortably warm against her skin. She pressed her palm to the rough bark of a maple and leaned against it.

Up the block, a car engine coughed to life, but Eleanora ignored it. Her attention was solely on Lady, who'd stopped to clean herself right there in the middle of the gravel-strewn road.

"Eleanora, hello there!" a familiar voice called out.

Eleanora momentarily shifted her gaze away from Lady to see a sweat-suited Helen Evans walking toward her up the sidewalk. But she neither answered nor waved.

Instead, she took in a deep breath and stepped into the street.

The squeal of tires filled her ears, and she froze like a deer caught in headlights as a car came out of nowhere and bore down on her.

"Eleanora!"

A hand snatched at her, dragging her from harm's way just as the car screeched past, kicking up so much gravel and dust in its wake that it seemed to disappear in a puff of smoke like a magician's grand finale.

She clung to her rescuer, her heart pounding in her ears and pumping the blood far too quickly through her veins. Eleanora shuddered, looking up into the gently lined face framed by gray.

"Oh, God, Helen," she got out despite the dryness of her mouth, clinging to the woman's arms for strength. "I think someone's trying to kill me."

Chapter 1

"I'M SORRY. I was looking for my friend Jean, but I must've stumbled into Julia Child's kitchen by mistake."

"Oh, Helen, stop it." Jean Duncan blushed and threw up a hand, as if to dismiss the thinly veiled compliment. "I'm just trying out a few things, experimenting, if you will."

"Pretty good-smelling experiments," Helen said and closed the screen door behind her. She entered the room, inhaling the mingling of scents, and leaned her hands against the stretch of countertop to survey the goings-on. Stainless steel bowls, measuring cups, and wooden cutting boards littered with the finely chopped remains of onions and chives filled every inch of space. Several copper pots topped the burners on the stove, their contents softly gurgling.

Helen glanced around her and caught sight of herself in the smoky glass of the built-in refrigerator. Sometimes it still surprised her to see a seventy-five-year-old woman in her reflection, albeit not a bad-looking one. Half the time she expected to see the dark-haired beauty she'd been in her youth, the energetic girl who'd graduated from Washington University when it still hadn't been fashionable to do so, who'd married at twenty-five and raised four children, all married now themselves.

She touched a hand to her unruly hair but dropped it again as the click of the oven door disrupted her thoughts.

She turned to Jean. "It looks like the Cordon Bleu around here," she remarked and sniffed. "Is that shrimp . . . oh, my, and Roquefort?"

Jean lifted the lid off a pot, allowing a cloud of steam to sneak out, wilting wisps of silver against her brow. "Right on both counts," she said. "Shrimp for the stuffed mushrooms and Roquefort for the chilled spinach dish." She settled the lid on the pot and gestured around her with a wooden spoon. "And, of course, there are onions and herbs for the liver pâté."

"Special occasion?"

"As a matter of fact, yes, very special." Jean snatched up a mixing bowl and hugged it to her belly, stirring its contents as she spoke. "I've finally decided to go for it."

"Go for what?" Helen tensed. At her age that could mean anything from buying a Miracle Ear to selling the house and moving into Shady Acres.

Jean's smile widened. "The catering business I've talked about starting ever since"—

she hesitated but quickly picked up where she'd left off—"ever since Jim died. Well, I've been moping around for more than a year, and this morning I woke up and decided to get on with my life, doing what I do best." She lifted her chin. "And that happens to be cooking for other people."

"That's marvelous," Helen told her, feeling as thrilled by the announcement as Jean did. Her friend looked good, better than she had in a long while. After the tragic car accident that had taken Jim's life nearly fifteen months before, Jean had put on weight, until she'd seemed a sad, bloated version of the lively woman Helen had remembered. Now the sixty-year-old widow was back to her fighting form, trim and full of energy in tan slacks and yellow sweater overlapped by a white apron. A bright scarf drew her hair off her shoulders into a ponytail. The smile on her mouth lit up her round face, giving it a rosy glow. Her hazel eyes looked bright, which cheered Helen to no end, as there'd been too many days when they'd filled with tears at the drop of a hat.

" . . . so that suits it, don't you think?"

Helen blinked, knowing she'd missed something. "I'm sorry, what did you say?"

"Just that I'm calling it The Catery," Jean replied, talking over her shoulder as she added eggs and onions to the goose liver. "You like it? Or is it, I don't know, too simple?"

"I've always liked simple."

"Good. Because I've already had some little deli containers made up with the name. I thought I'd get a few samples around, you know, to the Ladies Civic Improvement League and such."

"Speaking of the LCIL," Helen said, an idea cooking in her brain, "the annual luncheon's just about a month away, and I don't believe anyone's been hired to do the food yet."

"No, they haven't. I checked," Jean remarked and tapped a spoon in the air. "But wait'll I show them what I've got in mind," she said and grinned. Then she fixed her attention on the ingredients for her pâté de foie gras.

"Well, you've got my vote anyway," Helen told her. "The glop they served last year tasted like it was catered by the bait shop."

"Oh, Helen!"

"Well, it's true," she said, tapping a finger to her chin as an idea popped up. "The LCIL has a board meeting in the morning. It could help your cause if you showed up with some of your goodies."

"That's perfect." Jean's eyes widened. "Any suggestions?"

"It all looks good," Helen admitted, reaching over a colander filled with huge mushrooms to snatch a cheese puff from a batch not long out of the oven. She popped it into her mouth, chewing slowly, her eyes closing as she bit into the olive at the center. Was that paprika, she wondered, feeling her mouth tingle a bit and her cheeks flush. And cayenne pepper? She swallowed reluctantly and sighed aloud. When she opened her eyes, she found Jean watching her.

"Do I pass muster?" she asked, crossing her arms under her breasts. "Or should I quit now before I've started?"

Helen finished licking the tips of her fingers. Then she brushed her hands together, eyeing the rest of the cheese puffs. "My dear, I think you've found your calling."

Jean laughed. "I'll be the Mother Teresa of the card party set. Just give me a hungry bridge player, and I'll save her from starvation with a bowl of artichoke dip."

"Speaking of mothers," Helen began, wondering if now was the best time to broach the subject of Eleanora Duncan, what with Jean in such a good mood and all. But she swallowed any hesitation and plunged ahead. "I saw your former mother-in-law earlier when I was out for a walk, and she was—"

"Oh, I can only imagine what she was doing," Jean said, cutting her off. Her face tensed and the smile left her mouth, replaced by tight lips. "Knowing her, she was probably stealing candy from babies."

"Jean," Helen softly chided, but she couldn't blame her for her anger. Eleanora Duncan had as good as branded Jean a murderer after Jim died, and all because Jean had been at the wheel that rainy night of the accident. The feud that Eleanora had provoked with Jean made the one between the Hatfields and McCoys look like mere bickering in comparison.

Hardly a one of the two hundred inhabitants of tiny River Bend, Illinois, hadn't been a witness to Eleanora's lingering bitterness toward Jean. Having an eighty-year-old woman call her sixty-year-old daughter-in-law "Lucrezia Borgia" in the cereal aisle at the corner market wasn't something one easily forgot. But that wasn't the worst of it. Eleanora had made headlines when she'd used her considerable influence, the type only old money can buy, to push for a coroner's inquest of Jim's death. As expected, nothing had come of it except greater animosity between Eleanora and Jean.

Helen went around the island to where Jean leaned over the counter, furiously whisking a pair of eggs to their frothy deaths.

Helen touched her arm, and Jean let out a cry of pain. Helen took the bowl and whisk from her and set them aside. Then she picked up Jean's hands and held them tightly. "She's an old woman who wanted someone to blame, and you happened to be it."

Tears welled in Jean's eyes, though she blinked mightily, clearly determined not to cry. "She put me through hell, you know she did, as if what happened to Jim weren't enough. Like I didn't feel guilty enough without her adding to it."

"Someone nearly ran her over this morning," Helen said without further dillydallying.

Jean stared at her. "What?"

"I saw Eleanora step off the curb just as a car pulled into the street and almost hit her. It would have if I hadn't gotten to her first," Helen added.

"Maybe the driver didn't see her."

Helen shook her head. "The car sped up and never slowed down. It felt very deliberate."

"Oh." Jean paled, looking suddenly shaky. Helen guided her away from the mixing bowls and boiling shrimp and chopped onions, setting her down at the breakfast table. "Oh, my goodness," Jean said, her voice falling to a whisper. "Was she hit?"

"Not even scratched."

Jean wet her lips. "Did you recognize who was at the wheel?"

"It all happened so fast." Helen sighed, letting go of Jean's hands to pluck at several tufts of cat hair stuck to the legs of her pants. Amber's telltale yellow fur. She'd have to start brushing him now that spring had come, no matter how the old tom resisted.

"Is she okay?"

Helen glanced up, and her eyes met Jean's again. "As you'd expect, Eleanora was quite shaken."

Jean murmured, "The poor dear."

Within a few minutes, Eleanora Duncan had gone from being accused of stealing lollipops from babies to being "the poor dear." Helen smiled despite herself, thinking the scare Eleanora had endured this morning might actually result in something positive after all.

"Maybe I should"—Jean started to say but hesitated, squinting into the distance—"well, I'm probably the last person Eleanora wants to see, and I can't say I feel any different about her. But, like you said, Helen, she's had to deal with losing a husband and son within the past two years. I know she doesn't have many close friends despite all those committees she sits on. She's really all alone. Aw, hell," Jean groaned and let her head roll back. "I may be a fool, but I think I'll go by her place later on and take her something to eat. A little liver pâté, maybe some crab dip and stuffed mushrooms. What do you think?"

Helen stood and patted Jean's shoulder. "Sounds like a grand idea. With the way you cook, it might do a lot toward mending fences."

Jean got up as well and wiped her hands on her apron, nodding as if to convince herself it might possibly be true. She walked Helen out, holding the screen door wide with her hip. "Just so long as she doesn't accuse me of trying to poison her," she remarked before she waved Helen off.

"That's the spirit!" Helen laughed as she headed down the driveway toward the sidewalk.

About the Author

SUSAN McBRIDE is the *USA Today* bestselling author of *Blue Blood*, the first of the Debutante Dropout Mysteries. The award-winning series also includes *The Good Girl's Guide to Murder*, *The Lone Star Lonely Hearts Club*, *Night of the Living Deb*, and *Too Pretty to Die*. She's also the author of *The Truth about Love & Lightning*, *Little Black Dress*, and *The Cougar Club*, all Target Recommended Reads. She lives in St. Louis, Missouri, with her husband and daughter.

Visit Susan's web site at www.SusanMcBride.com for more info.

Visit www.AuthorTracker.com for exclusive information on your favorite HarperCollins authors.